DEEP SONG AND OTHER PROSE

ALSO BY FEDERICO GARCÍA LORCA

Five Plays: Comedies and Tragicomedies
Selected Poems
Three Tragedies

FEDERICO GARCÍA LORCA

DEEP SONG

AND OTHER PROSE

Edited and translated by Christopher Maurer

A NEW DIRECTIONS BOOK

Grateful acknowledgment is made to the editors and publishers of the following journals in which the translations of some of these essays first appeared: *Antaeus, Grove, Nebula,* and *The Niagara Magazine.*

Thanks are also due to Cambridge University Press for permission to reprint from Edward Meryon Wilson's English translation of *The Solitudes of Don Luis de Góngora.*

Manufactured in the United States of America
First published clothbound and as New Directions Paperbook 503 in 1980
Published simultaneously in Canada by George J. McLeod, Ltd., Toronto

Library of Congress Cataloging in Publication Data

García Lorca, Federico, 1898–1936.
Deep song and other prose.
(A New Directions Book)
Includes bibliographical references.
CONTENTS: Elegy for María Blanchard.—On lullabies.—Deep song. [etc.]
I. Maurer, Christopher. II. Title.
PQ6613.A763A258 1980 868'.6209 80-394
ISBN 0-8112-0764-1
ISBN 0-8112-0768-4 pbk.

New Directions Books are published for James Laughlin
by New Directions Publishing Corporation,
80 Eighth Avenue, New York 10011

CONTENTS

ACKNOWLEDGMENTS

I am deeply indebted to Margarita Ucelay of Barnard College for her patient help on these translations. I am also grateful to Isabel García Lorca, Jorge Guillén, José Luis Guerrero, the staffs of the Biblioteca Nacional, the Hemeroteca Nacional, and Hemeroteca Municipal, Madrid, and especially to Mario Hernández, editor of *Trece de Nieve,* for making it possible to correct the Spanish text of some of the lectures in this collection. All readers of Lorca's prose are indebted to Marie Laffranque, who rescued so much of it from oblivion.

Parts of this book appeared previously in *Antaeus, Grove, Niagara,* and *Nebula.*

This translation is for my father.

C.M.

INTRODUCTION

These are lectures, poetry readings, and occasional talks by Federico García Lorca. He gave them in Spain and the Americas during the last fourteen years of his life, and today they are the best spiritual portrait we have of him, apart from the poems and plays—for no matter what he happens to be lecturing about, Lorca is always . . . *himself*. He is always thinking about his roots and his part in a tradition far older than he, and in these lectures he reveals the ancient sources of his art.

The very existence of these lectures, and the fact that Lorca wrote few essays, is significant. From the start he mistrusted print. His creative powers were most stimulated in the presence of *listeners,* not future readers, and he was well known as a poet before he ever published a book. He once said, without exaggerating very much, that all of his manuscripts had been taken from him forcibly by editors and friends. When his poems and plays were printed he considered them "dead on the page," but when he read them to others he could make them live and protect them—"against incomprehension, dilletantism, and the benevolent smile." From early childhood he longed for the stage, but he was never completely at home there, and never completely able to make his work understood. (He surprised his audiences by appearing on stage in overalls or sweaters and unpressed trousers.) His early verse is not especially difficult, but when he returned from New York in 1930 with far more enigmatic poems he must have found that hardly anyone was able to follow them. Before reading his work to a large group of people in Barcelona in 1935 he said:

> I am a little afraid that my poems will be too personal or too obscure or too plain for you (plain because they have none of that musical leafiness that goes into the ears but never reaches the marrow of the emotions). I am afraid that beneath this high ceiling they will stiffen and shudder like the dirty cats stoned to death by children on the outskirts of villages.

So Lorca's lectures grew from an innate love of the stage and the yearning to make others understand his work.

Actually, only two chapters of this book are poetry readings. Several of the lectures concern folk art, which influenced Lorca more deeply and naturally than it did any other modern Spanish poet. "On Lullabies" describes the first awakening of a poet's sensibility, drawing much upon Lorca's own memories of childhood. The child lives, he writes,

> in an inaccessible poetic world that neither rhetoric nor the pandering imagination nor fantasy can penetrate. A flat surface, its nerve centers exposed, of horror and keen beauty, where a snow-white horse, half nickel and half smoke, falls suddenly injured, a swarm of furious bees at its eyes.

This is just the world Lorca wanted to create in his poems and plays—a separate world alien to everyday logic. One of his favorite lullabies is about a man ("*that* man") who leads his horse to the water without the horse ever drinking. The child must wonder *why.* Just as we are meant to wonder why

> A thousand crystal tambourines
> were wounding the dawn

and why

> The dawn of New York weeps
> up and down the long stairways
> searching among the edges
> for spikenards of sharp anguish.

"Only mystery makes us live. Only mystery," Lorca wrote at the foot of one of his sketches. And this is part of his esthetic credo.

In "Deep Song" ("cante jondo"), as in the lullabies, what interests him is the emotional intensity of the lyrics, an intensity born of Andalusian fatalism, the "pena" (pain, grief) that fills his own life and art.

The "Elegy for María Blanchard" shows Lorca characteristically defending a hunchback against her enemies. He defends the painter just as (in the *Gypsy Ballads* and *A Poet in New York*) he had defended Gypsies and blacks, whose spiritual treasures he had contrasted to the poverty of urban white civilization. Lorca feared that both of these peoples would enslave themselves to the whites, by "making theater of themselves" and selling them their music and their dance, the "quintessential expression of their pain." No doubt his own condition—his sexual abnormality and his being a born poet in a country unkind to its creators—made him long to understand the human condition of those who suffer: "I am used to suffering from things that people do not understand, do not even suspect. Being born in Granada," he once said, "has given me a sympathetic understanding of those who are persecuted—the Gypsy, the black, the Jew, the Moor which all Granadans have inside them."

In "Conversation with Bagaría" and "Holy Week in Granada" Lorca is careful to distinguish between two Granadas: on the one hand, the eternal city whose "silence and spiritual density" had made him "the creature I am—a poet from birth, unable to help it"; and on the other hand, the "poor, cowardly, narrow-minded city, inhabited at present by the worst bourgeoisie in all Spain." The first Granada, "withdrawn into herself, with no other escape than her deep natural port of stars," is a city "apt for rhythm and echo, the marrow of music," where Lorca learned his own deep song. The other Granada is filled with the "rotten" Philistines Lorca poked fun at as a young man, the sort of people who made Spanish life impossible for María Blanchard and made Lorca himself exclaim, when he was twenty, "Our aurora of peace and love will never come till we respect beauty and stop ridiculing those who sigh passionately after her. Unfortunate, illiterate country where it is laughable to be a poet!"

Here are the lectures of a young man discovering his own genius, showing it off a bit, and rebelling against Philistinism, pedantry, rhetoric, and those who speak "without energy and without the force of love." Addressing himself to the capital themes of human life—love, artistic creation, death—Lorca wanted to be *simple,* simple as the earth and the songs and plants that grow out of it. We get a good glimpse of him, in his early days as a "propagandista of poetic feeling," in a letter to Jorge Guillén of 1926:

> My lecture on Góngora was fun for the audience because I set out to *explain* the *Solitudes,* so that they would understand them and not be brutes . . . and they did! At least that is what they said. I have worked on it for three months. I will make a copy and send it to you. You tell me, *as a teacher,* what critical blunders it contains.
>
> But it was *serious.* My voice was another. It was a serene voice, full of *years* . . . the ones I am! It pained me a little to see that I am capable of lecturing without poking fun at the audience. I am becoming serious. I have many moments of pure sadness. At times I am surprised to see that I am *intelligent.* Old age!

Rafael Alberti has said that among the poets of the Generation of '27, he and Lorca were the ones most like toreros—each with his following, each proud of being able to move his audience. After giving a lecture in Granada on modern painting in 1928, Lorca wrote to a friend: "When I showed slides of Miró's paintings and praised them, things began to get ugly. But I dominated the audience. I even made them applaud." That is Lorca the matador (he even began one speech by hoping to "dar una estocada," i.e., "go straight to the theme and quickly master it, without lingering over what is merely accessory and decorative"). But it is better to compare him with a singer of deep song. Not only because he himself sang the musical parts of some of the lectures (the one on lullabies, another on Granadan folk songs, entitled "How a City Sings from November to November"), but because of the intimacy he sought with his audience, the many-headed monster he both needed and feared. The cantaor Don Antonio Chacón used to ask, before beginning to sing, "¿Los señores saben escuchar?" ("Do you know how to listen?"). Lorca would begin *his* lectures with a moment of intense concentration, like this:

> I want to summon up all the good will, all the purity of intention I have, because like all true artists I yearn for my poems to reach your hearts and cause the communication of love among you, forming the marvelous chain of spiritual solidarity that is the chief end of any work of art.

At times, before beginning to read, he invoked a chthonic spirit which he called the "duende." Only with the duende's help, he said, would audiences ever succeed at the "hard task of understanding metaphor" and be able "to hunt, at the speed of the voice, the rhythmic design of the poem." With the duende, he thought, one can be *sure* of being loved and understood.

The duende (from *duen de casa,* "lord of the house") is a Spanish household spirit fond of hiding things, breaking dishes, causing noise, and making a general nuisance of himself. In folk tales he is a little boy or very old man, appearing out of nowhere to help others or play tricks on them (there are two childlike duendes in Lorca's play *The Love of Don Perlimplín*). But in Andalusia the word duende is also applied to the ineffable, mysterious charm of certain gifted people, especially flamenco singers. The Andalusians say that a cantaor *has* duende.

During a trip to Argentina and Uruguay in 1933–34, Lorca devoted an entire lecture to the duende, included here. In it he describes (and avoids defining) not the poltergeist or dwarf of Spanish tradition but a protean earth spirit with three important traits: irrationality, demonism, and fascination with death. "Play and Theory of the Duende" is an entertainment; Ben Belitt calls it a *divertissement.* But it is something more—Lorca's attempt to come to grips with an eternal artistic problem that had troubled him from early youth: a simultaneous longing for form and respect for chaos (for the unknown, for what seems, or *is,* beyond form, beyond human art). The lecture on the duende is foreshadowed in the parable of the nocturnal hunting trip (p. 72) in the speech on Góngora. Lorca had praised Góngora's power of curbing his own imagination and of rejecting "the jewels which his own genius happens to place in his hands—the ugliness that comes to [other poets] through lack of serenity and self-love." A modern poet, tormented by thoughts of death, by everyday life, Lorca had looked into Góngora's green eternal world—free from anguish—had marveled at his "classic learning, which gave him faith in himself," and had had thoughts of emulating him. Now, years later, he suspects that the greatest poetry lies elsewhere. Góngora had built himself a rainproof "tower of gems and invented stones," but it occurred to Lorca that inspired poets ought to live closer to the earth and to the elements, their feet planted firmly on the ground, or even *in* it, "up to the waist in mud," as he told Bagaría. A year or so after he first lectured on Góngora, he was already having second thoughts. Asked for his esthetic creed, Lorca told a newspaperman in 1928:

> My only creed is to work hard. A return to inspiration, pure instinct, the poet's only reason. I cannot bear logical poetry. We've already given Góngora his due. Passion and instinct. For the time being.

"The true fight is with the duende," Lorca declared in Buenos Aires. And yet it is wrong to understand this lecture (as Belitt does) as Lorca's "case for the mantic in art." Lorca's solution is a more dialectical one. He says that the artist must *fight* the duende, hand to hand—i.e., he must fight his own irrationality, his own demonism, and his own death. Inspired art is born of that struggle. That is what Lorca told the poet Gerardo Diego in 1932:

> If it is true that I am a poet by the grace of God—or of the devil—I am also a poet by virtue of technique and effort, and knowing exactly what a poem is.

Craving and self-restraint are the systole and diastole of Lorca's prose. At times (but not often) he is obscure and chaotic. The author who writes incessantly and publishes little risks having his creations breed among themselves and of writing what W. H. Auden has called "woozy prose"—such writers are "too dependent upon some private symbolism of [their] own to be altogether comprehensible to others." For example:

> As simply as possible, in the register of my poetic voice that has neither the glow of woods [woodwinds?] nor bends of hemlocks, nor sheep who suddenly turn into knives of irony, I shall try to give you a simple lesson in the hidden spirit of disconsolate Spain. (p. 42).

Then too, Lorca occasionally imitates Góngora in alluding to myths "obliquely" and "showing just one aspect of them" (see p. 77). When he says, in the lecture on lullabies, that the mother "sits as though at an angle over the water, feeling herself spied upon by a severe critic of her voice," perhaps he is thinking of Narcissus (the mother) staring at his reflection in a pool of water (the child's eyes). In the earlier prose there are some startling Góngoristic periphrases, like this image of a virgin:

> In Orense another lullaby is sung, by a girl whose breasts, as yet blind, await the slippery murmur of her cloven apple.

Lorca thought by metaphor—he could not stop creating metaphors, some good, some bad. In fact, he was never able to read the very same lecture twice. In our version of "Deep Song," for example, he says that pain is "a dark woman wanting to catch birds in nets of wind." In another version, known only through newspaper accounts, he calls her a "brown little girl sitting in the dark, wearing green shoes that pinch her heart." Lovely images! But those green shoes do not fit—Lorca must have gone to the "nocturnal hunt" and found them hanging on a tree. Who else would have noticed them?

Perhaps only about a fourth of Lorca's prose is offered here. I hope that this book will do him justice. It does bring him back to have him put his own work into context and read his poems for us. Clumsily, I have tried to imitate his voice. Of course, this is not enough; to understand poetry, Lorca once said, "we need four white walls and a silence where the poet's voice can weep and sing."

—CHRISTOPHER MAURER

DEEP SONG AND OTHER PROSE

ELEGY FOR MARÍA BLANCHARD

LADIES AND GENTLEMEN:

I have come here neither as critic nor as connoisseur of the work of María Blanchard.[1] I am here as the friend of a shade—a sweet shade I have never seen, but who has spoken to me through certain mouths and certain cloudless landscapes where there was neither a stealthy footstep nor a cornered, frightened little animal. No one who knows me can have suspected María Gutiérrez Cueto was a friend of mine. I have never spoken of her, and when hearing about her from others, I used to turn my eyes away, as though distracted, and sing a little—people ought not to know that a poet is a man who is always—because of everything!—about to cry.

"Did you know María Blanchard? Tell me . . ."

One of the first paintings I saw as I was on the threshold of adolescence, going through that dramatic dialogue between peach fuzz and family mirror, was by María. Four bathers and a faun. The energetic color (laid on with a palette knife), the ease of composition, and the perfect fit of all her materials made me think of a tall María, dressed in scarlet, opulent and tenderly vulgar as an Amazon.

All boys carry a little white notebook they open only in the moonlight in which to take down the names of women they do not know but would like to carry to a bedroom of moss and illuminated snails in some lofty tower. Wedekind describes this very well, and Juan Ramón Jimenez' great lunar poetry is full of these women who come crazily to the window to give all the boys that come near them a bitter shot of pure hemlock.

When I took out my little book and began to write down María's name, and the name of her horse, they told me: "She is a hunchback."

Whoever has spent his youth in a city as socially barbarous as Granada was in my day must surely begin to think all women either impossible or stupid. A phrenetic fear of sex and a terror of "what people will say" used to turn girls into strolling automatons, under the watchful eyes of those big-bottomed "mamás" who wear men's shoes and grow little hairs on the side of their chins.

As an adolescent I had tenderly imagined María might not laugh at me for playing boring classical pieces on the piano nor for attempting poems. She was an artist; at least she would not laugh the repugnant laugh that boys and girls and their dirty mamas and papas reserved for purity and poetic wonder in the pitiable Spain of '98.

But poor María fell down the stairs, and her crooked shoulder became a target for paper dolls hanging from strings, for lottery tickets and ridicule.[2]

Who pushed her? She was after all pushed, and *someone* was to blame—God, the devil, someone anxious to contemplate, through poor windowpanes of flesh, the perfection of a beautiful soul.

María Blanchard came from a fantastic family. Her father was a gentleman from Santander, her mother a refined lady with such powers of fantasy she was almost a prestidigitator. When the mother was very old, some children I knew went to keep her company. Stretched out on her bed, she would pull grapes, pears, and sparrows from under her pillow. She was always losing the keys; she had to look for them every day, and would find them in the strangest places—under the bed or inside the mouth of her dog. María's father would go out riding and return without his horse, the horse having fallen asleep and the father having thought it a shame to wake him. He organized great hunting parties without guns, and often forgot the name of his wife. No one noticed María, and as time went flowing by she grew smaller and smaller. A hand took her by the feet and began to immerse her head in her body, till she looked like the jumping jack *"Don Nicanor que toca el tambor."*[3]

It was around this time, which coincides with the final apotheosis of Rubén Dario, that I saw the only portrait I have ever seen of María—a sad caricature (I do not know who drew it) showing her beside the Mexican painter Diego Rivera, her true antithesis, a sensual artist who is now (as María rises to heaven) painting in gold and kissing the terrible navel of Plutarco Elías Calles.

This is when María is living in Madrid, sheltering people in her house—a Russian, a Chinese, whoever happens to knock at her door. She has already been seized by that delicate mystical delirium that crowned her stay in Paris with the cold camelia blossoms of Zurbarán.

María Blanchard's struggle was as hard, prickly, and stubborn as a branch of evergreen oak. Instead of resenting it, she was sweet, godly, and virgin. Without wanting to, her body, the body of a buffoon from the beggar's opera, brought downpours of laughter, but María endured. Her first exhibitions were ridiculed; she endured that too, with the serenity another great painter, Barradas (now dead and an angel), showed when the public smashed his pictures. He replied with the recondite silence of clover or of a persecuted creature.

With the patience of a nurse, María put up with her friends—the Russian who talked of golden coaches or counted emeralds in the snow, or the giant fatman Diego Rivera, who thought people and things were spiders that were about to eat him and threw his shoes at the lightbulbs and each day broke the bathroom mirror. She put up with others, too, and in the end, she was left alone, entirely bereft of human communication—so intensely alone that she had to search within herself for an invisible fatherland where her wounds might run and coalesce with the whole stylized world of pain.

As time passed, her soul made itself purer; her acts became more responsible, more transcendent. Her painting kept to the same masterly road, from the famous picture of *The First Communion* till her last scenes of mothers and children. Tormented by a superior morality, she gave away her paintings for half the price offered her, while mending her own shoes with beautiful humility.

Christ's life and passion grew more luminous in her daily life, and like the great Falla she used them as touchstone, dogma, and consolation. Not with the affected devotion of an old lady, and not with a political, anti-Christian cross hanging pornographically on her bosom, but in practice. With serious pain. With charity. With intelligence. The most Spanish thing about María Blanchard was the way she hunted Christ and captured Him, a God and a supremely real, great man. Her search was far different from that of, say the fantastical Catherine of Siena, who came to be married with the Christ child and exchanged not rings but hearts with him.

María's search was a dry one—no angels, no miracles. It was quicklime, pure earth.

No one caressed her monstrous waist, save that great dead hand, just unnailed from the Cross and still spurting blood.[4] This was the arm that lovingly pushed her down the stairs to take her as His bride and His delight, and helped her in terrible "childbirth" when the huge dove of her soul could hardy squeeze through her sunken mouth.[5] I am not telling you this for you to meditate upon its truth or falsehood. It is myth that creates the world. Without Neptune the sea would be deaf, and the waves owe half of their fascination to the human invention of Venus.

Dear María Blanchard. Two points.[6] A world, the dark pillow on which your head is resting.

Your very body mathematically showed the angel's struggle with the devil. When children saw you from behind they would shout, "The witch! There goes the witch!" Yet whenever a boy saw your head appear in one of those tiny Castilian windows he would shout, "A fairy!" María—witch or fairy—you set a fine example of grief and of spiritual lucidity. All praise you now. Critics praise your work and friends praise your life. I would like to be gallant to you, both as a man and as a poet. I would like to make this modest elegy say something very old, as old as the word "serenade," though naturally with no irony at all. And without using the language of the man who is sophisticated and "modern." In all sincerity. I have been calling you a hunchback, but I have said nothing of your pretty eyes, which filled with tears as a thermometer pulses full of mercury. Nor have I mentioned your hands, the hands of a maestro. And I want to speak of your wonderful long hair. I want to praise it. You had a head of hair so beautiful and so generous that it wanted to cover your body as the palm tree covered the Child you loved on His flight into Egypt. You were a hunchback. But men understand little. I want to tell you, María Blanchard, as a friend of your shade: you had the most beautiful head of hair there has ever been in Spain.

ON LULLABIES

LADIES AND GENTLEMEN:

In this lecture I am not trying, as in former ones, to define, but to emphasize.[1] I want to suggest, not to delineate. To animate, in the exact sense of the word. To wound drowsy birds. To direct into this or that dark corner light reflected from a distant cloud, and to hand out some pocket mirrors to the ladies who are present.

I have wanted to go down to the rushy shore. Under the yellow tiles. To the outskirts of villages, where the tiger eats little children. I am far now from the poet who looks at his watch, who struggles with the statue, with dream, and with anatomy. I have fled all my friends and am going off with the little boy who eats green fruit and watches the ants devour the bird run over by the automobile.

You will find me on the purest streets of the village, in the wandering wind and stretching light of the melodies that Rodrigo Caro called "reverend mothers of all songs." You will find me wherever, a boy's ear opens, rosy and tender—wherever there opens the tiny white ear of the girl who awaits, full of fear, the pin that will bore a hole for the earring.

On all my walks through Spain, whenever I grew a little tired of cathedrals, dead stones, and soulful landscapes, I have tried to search for the perpetually living elements where the minute does not freeze, elements that live a tremulous present. Among the infinite number that exist, I have followed two: songs and sweets. While a cathedral is always fastened to its own epoch, giving the landscape a ceaseless expression of yesterday, a song leaps out of that yesterday into our own moment. Live and pulsing as a frog, brought forth like some new shrub, the song brings us living light of old hours, thanks to the breath of the melody.

All travelers are lost. To know the Alhambra of Granada, for example, before touring its rooms and courtyards, it is very useful, very pedagogical to eat the delicious "alfajor" of Zafra, or the nuns' "tortas alajú," the taste and fragrance of which give us the authentic temperature of the palace when it was alive—the ancient light, the cardinal points of the temperament of its court.

In melody as in sweets, history's emotion and permanent light take refuge, free of facts and dates. Love and the gentle breeze of our country are contained in songs or in the rich paste of almond nougat as they can never be in stones, bells, folk with character, or even language, and thus bring us living life from dead epochs.

The melody, much more than the text of a song, defines a region's geographic traits and the line of its history, vividly distinguishing moments in a profile that time has erased. After all, a ballad is not perfect unless it has its own melody to make it palpitate and give it blood and a severe or erotic air for its characters to move around in.

The throbbing melody, with its structure of nerve centers and little blood vessels, can infuse living, historic warmth into texts that are either empty or worthless except as rude evocations.

Before going ahead, I ought to say that I am not trying to settle these matters once and for all. I am on a poetic plane where the yes and no of things are equally true. Were you to ask me, "Is a moonlit night of one hundred years ago identical to a moonlit night of ten years ago?" I could demonstrate (as could any other poet who is master of his craft) that it was. But with the same ring of indisputable truth, I could also prove that it was not. I am trying to avoid the sort of ugly erudite data that tire out audiences; it is emotional data I shall try to emphasize. You are surely more interested in knowing whether a melody can give birth to a finely sifted, soporific breeze, or whether a song can place a simple landscape before the child's newly jelled eyes, than in knowing whether the melody is of the seventeenth century or whether it is written in 3/4 time, information the poet ought to know but not repeat and which is, after all, within reach of anyone who dedicates himself to these matters.

Some years ago, as I was strolling through the outskirts of Granada, I heard a village woman singing her child to sleep. I had always been aware of the keen sadness of our country's cradle songs, but never so vividly as then. As I approached the singer to take down the words, I saw that she was a pretty Andalusian, a happy woman without the slightest twinge of melancholy. But a living tradition was at work in her: she was faithfully obeying an order, as though listening to the ancient, imperious voices that went skittering through her blood. Since then I have tried to collect lullabies from all parts of Spain. I wanted to know how the women of my country put their children to sleep, and after a while I found that Spain uses its very saddest melodies and most melancholy texts to darken the first sleep of her children. By no means does this happen in just one model, one song, isolated in this or that region. Every region accentuates its own poetic character, its depth of sadness, in this kind of song, from Asturias and Galicia to Andalusia and Murcia, with saffron and the recumbent mode of Castile between them.[2]

There exists a tranquil, monotonous European cradle song to which the child can contentedly surrender himself, developing all his aptitude for sleep. France and Germany provide some good examples, and among us the Basques sound the European note with lullabies of the same lyricism as the Northern songs, full of tenderness and lovable simplicity.

The European cradle song tries only to put the child to sleep, not, as the Spanish one, to wound his sensibility at the same time.

The rhythm and monotony of the lullabies I call European can make them seem melancholy, but they are not inherently so, only accidentally, as a jet of water or trembling leaves can be at any given moment. We should not confuse monotony with melancholy. The most succulent part of Europe[3] hangs heavy gray curtains in front of its children to make them sleep peacefully. Double virtue of wool and sheepbell. With the greatest finesse.

The Russian cradle songs that I know, though they have the oblique, sad Slavic sound—cheekbone and distance—of all Russian music, do not have the cloudless clarity, the steep obliquity, and emotional simplicity that characterize the Spanish ones. The child is able to bear the sadness of the Russian lullaby as one bears a day of mist beyond the windowpanes. Not in Spain. Spain is the country of profiles. There are no smudgy limits one can cross to flee to the other world. Everything is delineated and bounded very exactly. A dead man is deader in Spain than in any other part of the world. Whoever wants to jump into dream wounds his feet on the blade of a barber's razor.

Do not think I am here to talk about "Black Spain," "Tragic Spain," etc. etc., worn out clichés now devoid of literary value. But the landscape of those regions that most tragically represent Spain, the regions where Castilian is spoken—that landscape has the same harsh accent, the same dramatic originality, the same lean air as the songs that sprout in it. We must always admit that Spain's beauty is not serene, sweet, or restful; it is burning, excessive, scorched, and sometimes completely orbitless. Beauty without the light of an intelligent scheme to lean on. Beauty blinded by its own brilliance, dashing its head against the walls.

Surprising rhythms, melodic constructions full of transcendent mystery and ancientness are to be found in the Spanish countryside. But we will never find one elegant rhythm, one self-conscious rhythm, one rhythm that develops with loving serenity even though springing from the tip of a flame. And yet within this tempered sadness and rhythmic furor, Spain has happy songs, fun and jokes, songs of delicate eroticism and enchanting madrigals. Why then does she save to put her children to sleep the bloodiest songs, those least suited to a child's delicate sensibility?

We should not forget that the cradle song is invented (as its words show) by wretched women whose children are a burden, a cross that is often too heavy for them to carry. Each child is a grief rather than a joy. And naturally the women cannot help singing to them (even though they love them) of their own weariness with life. There are good examples of this attitude, this resentment of the child who has arrived—even though his mother wanted him—at the worst possible moment. In Asturias, in the village of Navia, this lullaby is sung:

Este niñín que teño nel collo	This little boy on my lap
e d'un amor que se ṭṣama Vitorio,	is from a lover named Vitorio.
Dios que modeu, ṭṣéme llungo,	May God who has given him to me
por non andar con Vitorio nel collo.	take Vitorio from my lap.

And its melody is in tone with the utter misery of the words.

Poor women feed this melancholy bread not only to their own children, they also bring it into the houses of the rich. The rich child listens to the lullaby of the poor woman, who gives him, in her pure sylvan milk, the marrow of the country.

For a long time now these wet nurses, maids, and other domestic servants have been doing the important job of carrying the ballad, the song, and the story into the houses of aristocrats and bourgeoises. Rich children know of Gerineldo, Don Bernardo, Tamar, and the Lovers of Teruel[4] thanks to the admirable wet nurses and domestics who descend from the mountains or from far up the river to give us our first lesson in Spanish history and brand our flesh with the harsh Iberian motto: "Alone you are; alone you will live."

Different factors, all of them important, summon the child to sleep. Naturally we count on the co-operation of fairies. It is they who bring the anemones and the right temperature. The mother and the song add the rest.

Those of us who consider the child to be the chief spectacle of all nature and think that no flower, no silence, no number can compare with him, have often observed how just before going to sleep and without anyone's having attracted his attention he suddenly turns his head from the starchy breast of the nanny (that quivering little volcano of milk and blue veins) and fixes his gaze on the room made silent for his sleep.

"She's here!" I always say. And sure enough, she is.

In 1917 I had the great luck to see a fairy in the room of a little boy, a cousin of mine. She was gone in a hundredth of a second, and yet I saw her. Well, I saw her as we see pure things on the very edge of the circulation of our blood—out of the corner of the eye, as the great poet Juan Ramón Jiménez saw the sirens while returning from America. He saw them just as they submerged.[5] Anyway, this fairy was clinging to a curtain, utterly splendid, as though dressed in passementerie. But I cannot remember her size or expression. Nothing would be easier for me to invent her to my own taste, but that would be blatant poetic deception, not poetic creation, and I do not want to deceive anyone. I speak neither ironically nor in jest, but with the deeply rooted faith of the poet, the child, and the complete fool.[6] In mentioning fairies I have done my duty as propagandist of the poetic feeling that is nearly lost today thanks to literary men and intellectuals who have attacked it with the powerful human weapons of irony and analysis.

Once the fairies have created the right atmosphere, two rhythms are needed, the physical rhythm of the cradle or chair and the intellectual rhythm of the melody. The mother fits together these rhythms, one for the body and one for the hearing, using various measures and silences.

She blends them till she finds the very tone capable of enchanting the child.

It makes no difference whether the song has words. Sleep comes even when there is only rhythm and the vibration of the voice against that rhythm. The perfect lullaby would be the seesaw repetition of two notes for as long as possible. But no mother wants to be a snake charmer, though her technique is basically the same.

She needs the words to keep the child hanging on her lips, and as sleep approaches she enjoys not only singing nice things but also submerging the child in crude reality and imbuing him with the drama of the world.

So then, the words of the song run counter to sleep and its gentle river. The words evoke emotions in the child, doubt and terror against which the melody's blurry hand, the hand that combs and tames the prancing little horses in the child's eyes, must struggle.

Let us not forget that the main purpose of the lullaby is to put to sleep the child who is not sleepy. There are songs for the daytime and for the hours when the child feels like playing. In Tamames this one is sung:

Duérmete, mi niño,	Sleep, my child,
que tengo quehacer,	I have things to do:
lavarte la ropa,	wash your clothes
ponerme a coser.	and sew.

And at times the mother carries on a real battle that ends in spankings, crying, and finally, sleep. Notice that the lullaby is almost never sung to a newborn child. A newborn child can be entertained by a sketchy melody hummed under the breath, the physical rhythm of the cradle being more important. The lullaby requires a spectator who can understand its plot and take pleasure in the anecdote or character or landscape the song expresses. The child who is sung to already talks, is beginning to walk, and already knows the meaning of the words. Often he sings along.

In the silent moment of the song child and mother have a very delicate relationship. The child stays alert to protest the lyrics or liven up an overly monotonous rhythm. The mother sits as though at an angle over the water, feeling herself spied upon by a severe critic of her voice.[7]

We know that in one way or another all over Europe children are frightened by the "coco." Along with the "bute" and the Andalusian "marimanta," the coco forms part of a strange infantile world full of vague figures that rear up like elephants in the graceful fable of domestic spirits that still breathe in certain corners of Spain.[8]

The magic power of the coco lies precisely in his shadowiness. He wanders around the room but never shows himself. What is really charming is that he is just as shadowy, as unsketched, for everyone. We are dealing with a poetic abstraction, and for that reason the fear it causes is a cosmic fear, a fear around which the senses cannot place their safe bounds and objective walls, defending us amid the danger from greater dangers (greater because inexplicable). But no doubt the child tries to picture that abstraction, and very often he applies the word "coco" to this or that extraordinary form found in nature. The child is free to imagine the coco for himself, but whether or not he fears it depends upon his fantasy. He can even find the coco to be nice. I knew a little girl from Catalonia who could not be dragged away from an exhibition of Cubist paintings by my great friend from the Residencia, Salvador Dalí; that is how enthused she was by his papos and cocos, those huge, extraordinarily expressive squares of burning paint.

But Spain does not care too much for the coco. She prefers to scare her children with real beings. In the South the "bull" and the "Moorish Queen" are the real threats; in Castile the "she-wolf" and the "Gypsy woman." And in northern Burgos the "Aurora" is marvelously substituted for the coco. The same method of infusing silence is used in the most popular lullaby of Germany, where it is a sheep who comes to bite the child.[9] The concentration, the flight to another world, the yearning for shelter and surer limits that accompany the appearance of these real or imaginary beings, all this is a rather imprudent way to bring sleep. But this technique of fear is not all that common in Spain. She has other methods, some more refined and some more cruel.

Often the mother constructs an abstract, usually nocturnal landscape, and puts into it, as into an old play, one or two actors who do the simplest things, almost always with a touch of melancholy as beautiful as possible. The child is forced to imagine certain characters crossing this little stage set, and they loom large in the hot mists of sleeplessness.

This sort of lullaby has the gentlest lyrics; the child can travel through them with relative confidence. Andalusia has some beautiful specimens. These would be the most rational cradle songs of all, were it not for the melodies. The melodies have a dramatic intensity that is almost unthinkable considering their function. I have collected, in Granada, six versions of this lullaby:

A la nana, nana, nana,
a la nanita de aquel
que llevó el caballo al agua
y lo dejó sin beber.

Lullaby, lullaby
of that man who led
his horse to the water
and left him without drink.

In Tamames (Salamanca) there is this one:

Las vacas de Juana
no quieren comer;
llévalas al agua,
que querrán beber.

Juana's cows
don't want to eat;
take them to the water,
they want to drink.

In Santander this one is sung:

Por aquella calle a la larga
hay un gavilán *perdío*
que dicen que va a llevarse
la paloma de su *nío.*

Along that street
there is a lost hawk.
They say he will take
the dove from her nest.

And in Pedrosa del Principe (Burgos):

A mi caballo le eché
hojitas de limon verde
y no las quiso comer.

I gave my horse
leaves of green lemon,
and he would not eat them.

These four texts differ in sentiment and character, but they have the same ambience. The mother evokes a landscape, the simplest possible; then she sends a traveler through it, a man or woman whom she rarely names (I know of just two baptised characters in all the world of lullabies: Pedro Neilera, of Villa del Grado, who carries his bagpipes on a pole; and the delightful Galindo of Castile, who could not hold class because he beat his pupils without taking off his spurs).

The mother carries the child outside himself into the distance and returns him to her lap tired and ready for sleep. It is a little initiation into poetic adventure, the child's first steps through the world of intellectual representation. In this lullaby, the most popular cradle song of the kingdom of Granada,

Lullaby, lullaby
of that man who led

his horse to the water
and left him without drink[10]

the child enjoys the lyrical play of pure beauty before giving in to sleep. Silently, again and again, *that* man and his horse go down the road of dark boughs toward the river, and return to the spot where the song begins. The child will never see them face to face. In the penumbra of the lullaby he will only imagine *that* man's dark suit, his horse's shiny rump. The characters in these songs never show their faces. They must withdraw, must open the road toward places where the water is deeper and the bird has forever renounced her wings. But the melody makes *that* man and his horse intensely dramatic, and the strangeness of the man not watering his horse causes a rare and mysterious anguish.

In this type of song the child recognizes the character and sketches his profile according to his own visual experience, which is always greater than we suppose. He is forced to be a spectator and a creator at the same time. And what a marvelous creator! A creator with poetic feeling of the highest order. We have only to study the child's first games, before he is benighted by intelligence, to see that they are animated by planetary beauty and perfect simplicity. He discovers mysterious relations between things and objects that Minerva will never be able to decipher. With a button, a spool of thread, a feather, and the five fingers of his hand, the child builds a difficult world full of fresh resonances that sing and collide disturbingly, and happiness that need not be analyzed. The child understands much more than we think he does. He is in an inaccessible poetic world that neither rhetoric nor the pandering imagination nor fantasy can penetrate. A flat surface, its nerve centers exposed, of horror and keen beauty, where a snow-white horse, half nickel and half smoke, falls suddenly injured, a swarm of furious bees at its eyes.

Unlike ours, the child's creative faith is still unbroken, and he does not yet carry the seed of destructive reason. He is innocent and therefore wise. He understands better than we the ineffable key to poetic substance. At other times the mother goes on an adventure with her child. In the region of Guadix this song is sung:[11]

A la nana, niño mío,	Lullaby, my child,
a la nanita y haremos	oh we will build
en el campo una chocita	a hut in the country
y en ella nos meteremos.	and go inside.

The two of them depart. Danger is near. We must make ourselves smaller, tiny, and the walls of the little hut will touch our skin. Outside they are waiting to hurt us. We must live in a tiny place. If we can we will live inside an orange, you and me. Even better, inside a grape!

And sleep comes, brought on by just the opposite of the "distance" method. To put the child to sleep by putting a road in front of him is a little like hypnotizing a rooster with a line of white chalk. The second way, gathering up the child within himself, is much sweeter. His happiness is like that of watching a terrible flood from safe in the branch of a tree.

There are instances in Spain, in Salamanca and in Murcia, of the mother pretending to be a child.

Tengo sueño, tengo sueño,	I am sleepy, I am sleepy
tengo ganas de dormir.	how I want to go to sleep.
Un ojo tengo cerrado,	One of my eyes is closed,
otro ojo a medio abrir.	the other is half open.

Here the mother usurps the child's role so peremptorily that, lacking any defense, he is simply forced to sleep.

But the most complete, most widespread group of lullabies are those where the child is made the only actor. He is shoved into his own lullaby, dressed for the part, and given some unpleasant task. These are the most widely sung lullabies with the richest Spanish substance. The melodies are the most original of all and the most markedly indigenous.

The child is tenderly scolded and abused: "Go away, you're no child of mine, your mother is a Gypsy." Or, "Your mother isn't here, you have no cradle, you are as poor as Our Lord." And so on, always in that tone.

There is no longer any attempt to menace, frighten, or build a scene. Only to thrust the child inside the song, alone and unarmed, a defenseless little knight against the reality of the mother.

The child's reaction to this sort of lullaby is always protest, strong or weak according to his sensibility.

I have witnessed innumerable cases in my own large family where the child simply stopped the song. He cries, he kicks until the wet nurse changes the record, much to her disgust, and breaks into another song, in which the child's sleep is compared with the bovine blush of the rose.

In Trubia this "añada" is sung, a lesson in disillusionment:

Crióme mi madre	My mother raised me
feliz y contentu,	happy and content.
cuando me dormía	Rocking me to sleep
me iba diciendo:	she used to say
"¡Ea, ea, ea!,	"Lullaby, lullaby
tú has de ser marqués,	you must become a marquis
conde o caballeru";	a count or a gentleman."
y por mi desgracia	But alas, I learned
yo aprendí a "goẍeru."	to weave baskets.
Facía los "goẍos"	All during January
en mes de Ẍineru	I made baskets,
y por el verano	and during the summer
cobraba el dineru.	collected the money.
Aquí esta la vida	Such is the life
del pobre "goẍeru,"	of a basketmaker.
"¡Ea, ea, ea!" etc., etc.	"Lullaby, lullaby," etc., etc.

And now listen to this lullaby, sung in Cáceres, of rare melodic purity, which seems made to be sung to children who have no mother and whose lyrics are so severe, so ripe that it seems more like a song to die to than a song for our first sleep:[12]

Duérmete, ni niño, duérmete	Sleep, my child, sleep,
que tu madre no está en casa,	your mother's not at home.
que se la llevó la Virgen	The Virgin came and took her home
de compañera a su casa.	for a friend . . .

There are several songs of this sort in the north and west of Spain, where the lullaby acquires a crueler, more miserable tone.

In Orense another lullaby is sung, by a girl whose breasts, as yet blind, await the slippery murmur of her cloven apple:[13]

Ora, meu meniño, ora;	Now, now, child,
¿quen vos ha de dá la teta	who will give you suck?
se teu pai vai no muiño	Your father went to the mountain,
e tua mai na leña seca?	your mother to gather wood.

The women of Burgos sing:

Echate, niño, al ron ron,	Child, lie down and sleep,
que tu padre está al carbón	your father's getting coal.
y tu madre a la manteca	Your mother's at the churn
no te puede dar la teta.	and cannot give you suck.

These two lullabies are much alike. The venerable antiquity of both is obvious. The schemes of both of their melodies develop within a tetrachord. For simplicity and purity of design they are unrivaled in any songbook.

Particularly sad is the lullaby the Gypsies of Seville sing to their children. But I do not think it native to Seville. It is the one type I have presented that was influenced by the songs of the northern mountains and which has not the incorruptible melodic autonomy that each region develops. In all Gypsy songs we find a northern influence that comes by way of Granada. It was in Seville that this song was collected by a friend of great musical meticulousness, yet it seems to have been born in the valleys of the coastal mountain chain between Gibraltar and Alicante. In design it resembles this well-known song of Santander:

Por aquella vereda	Through that pasture
no pasa nadie,	nobody goes,
que murió la zagala	the shepherd girl died,
la flor del valle,	the valley's flower
la flor del valle,	the valley's flower,
sí, etc.	etc.

The Gypsies' song is one of those sad lullabies in which the child is left alone, though with great tenderness. It goes:

Este galapaguito	This little turtledove
no tiene madre,	has no mother.
lo parió una gitana,	A Gypsy bore him
lo echó a la calle.	and put him in the street.[14]

There is no doubt of its Northern or, better said, Granadan accent. I know the Granadan songs because I have myself collected them where, as in the songs' landscape, the snow is at peace with the fountain, the fern with the orange. But one must be careful about such statements. Years ago Manuel de Falla was saying that a certain song sung in the lowest villages of the Sierra Nevada on May Day was unquestionbly of Asturian origin. The different transcriptions we took to him strengthened his belief. But one day he himself heard it sung, and upon transcribing and studying it he saw that its ancient rhythm was epitritic and that it had nothing to do with typical Asturian tonality or meter. The transcriptions we had made had dislocated the rhythm and made the song "Asturian." No doubt Granada has many songs of Galician and Asturian tone because of the settlements of Asturians and Galicians in the mountains of the Alpujarra. But there are a thousand other influences difficult to detect through that terrible mask that hides everything, the mask of "regional character." How often it confuses and clouds the clues, which can then be deciphered only by technicians as deep as Falla, with his first-rate artistic intuition.

In the whole of Spanish folklore, with a few glorious exceptions, the matter of transcriptions is a terrible mess. Many songs now circulating in songbooks ought to be considered untranscribed. There is nothing so delicate as a rhythm, the base of all melody, and nothing more difficult than the voice of a people who divide each tone into thirds and even fourths which cannot be shown on the composer's stave. It is time to replace our imperfect songbooks with collections of gramophone records, indispensable to the scholar and the musician.

There are other cradle songs (one in Morón de la Frontera and another in Usana, the latter collected by the great Pedrell) of the same ambience as the lullaby of the little turtledove. But their melodies are much more sober, lean, and pathetic.

The most ardent lullaby of all, the most representative of Castile, is sung in Béjar. This one would ring like a gold coin if we dropped it on the rocky earth:

Duérmete, niño pequeño, duerme, que te velo yo; Dios te dé mucha ventura neste mundo engañador.	Sleep, little boy, sleep, for I am watching you. God give you much luck in this lying world.
Morena de las morenas la Virgen del Castañar; en la hora de la muerte ella nos amparará.	Darkest of all dark women the Virgen of Castañar at the hour of our death will help us.

In Asturias another añada is sung in which the mother complains about her husband in front of the child. Surrounded by drunken men in the close, rainy night of that country, the husband bangs open the door. The mother is rocking the child, a wound on her foot, a wound that bloodies the cruel, cruel hawsers of ships:[15]

Todos los trabayos son para las pobres muyeres aguardando por las noches que los maridos vinieren.	All the work falls to the poor women, who wait in the night for their men to come.
Unos veníen borrachos, otros veníen alegres; otros decíen: "Muchachos, vamos matar las muyeres."	Some arrive drunk, some a little tipsy, Others say, "Boys, let's kill our wives!"
Ellos piden de cenar, ellas que darles no tienen. "¿Qué ficiste los dos riales? Muyer, ¡qué gobierno tienes!" Etc., etc.	They ask for dinner, the women have nothing to give them. "But what did you do with the change? Woman, what a house you keep!" Etc., etc.

It would be difficult to find anywhere in Spain a sadder, more crudely salacious song than this. But we have yet to consider a truly extraordinary type of lullaby, examples of which are sung in Asturias, Salamanca, Burgos, and Leon. It belongs to no region in particular but circulates through the north and center of the Peninsula. It is the lullaby of the adulterous woman who arranges a rendezvous with her lover while singing to her child.

Its mysterious, ironic double entendre startles you every time you hear it. The mother scares the child with a man who is at the door and must not come in. The father is at home, and would not allow it. The Asturian variant says:

El que está en la puerta que no entre agora, que está el padre en casa del neñu que llora.	The man at the door must not come inside, at home is the father of the crying child.

Ea mi neñín, agora non,	Lullaby, my child, not now,
ea, mi neñín, que esta el papón.	not now, Big Daddy's here.
El que está en la puerta	The man at the door
que vuelva mañana,	must come back tomorrow;
que el padre del neñu	the child's father
está en la montaña.	will be in the mountains.
Ea, mi neñín, agora non,	Lullaby, my child, not now,
ea, mi neñín, que está el papón.	not now, Big Daddy's here.

The adultress's song that is sung in Alba de Tormes is more lyrical than the Asturian one, and its feelings are more guarded:

Palomita blanca	Little white bug
que andas a deshora	who comes at the wrong time,
el padre está en casa	at home is the father
del niño que llora.	of the crying child.
Palomita negra	Little black bug
de los vuelos blancos,	with snowy wings
está el padre en casa	at home is the father
del niño que canta.	of the child who sings.

The variant sung at Burgos, at Salas de los Infantes, is the most transparent of all:

Qué majo que eres,	How handsome you are,
qué mal que lo entiendes,	why don't you see
que está el padre en casa	that father's at home
y el niño no duerme.	and baby can't sleep.
Al mu mu	Lullaby
al mu mu del alma	lullaby, my soul,
¡que te vayas tú!	away with you!

It is a beautiful woman who sings these songs. The goddess Flora, with unsleeping breast apt for the head of the viper. Avid for fruit and clean of melancholy.[16] This is the only lullaby in which the child has no importance at all: he is a mere pretext.

I do not mean to say that all the women who sing these songs are adultresses. But yes, without knowing it they enter the ambit of adultery.

After all, that mysterious man at the door, the man who does not come in, is the man whose face is hidden under a big hat, the man dreamed about by every true, unbound woman.

I have tried to show you several sorts of songs that (except for Seville) answer to regional models characterized by the melodies. Songs that have never been influenced, fixed melodies ever unable to travel. The songs that travel are those whose feelings keep a certain peaceful balance, songs with a universal air. These are aseptic songs, quick to change their mathematical suit of rhythm, flexible in accent, and indifferent to the lyric temperature. Each region has a fixed, incorruptible melodic nucleus, and a true army of wandering songs that circulate wherever they can and die sunken in the farthest frontier of their influence.

There is a group of Asturian and Galician songs, moist and tinged with green, that descend to Castile, where they acquire rhythmic structure and get as far as Andalusia, where they take on the Southern manner and turn into the odd songs of the mountains of Granada.

The deep song's Gypsy "siguiriya," the purest expression of the Andalusian lyric, never breaks out of Jerez or Córdoba, but the "bolero," a neutral melody, is danced in Castile and even Asturias. Torner collected an authentic "bolero" in Llanes.

Day and night Galician "alalás" pound the walls of Zaragoza in vain, but we can hear the accents of the "muñeira" in the melodies of certain ritual dances and chants of the Gypsies of the South. "Sevillanas" that the Moors of Granada transported in one piece to Tunis undergo a complete change of rhythm and character on arriving in La Mancha, and they never succeed in crossing the Guadarrama.

By sea Andalusia influences the very lullabies of which I have spoken; but her influence never travels to the North, as it does in some other kinds of songs. The Andalusian style of lullaby colors the lower Levant and even the "vou-veri-vou" of the Balearics. Passing through Cadiz it reaches the Canaries, whose delicious "arrorró" is of undoubted Andalusian accent.

We could make a map of Spanish melodies and note on it a fusion of regions, an exchange of bloods and juices alternating with the systoles and diastoles of the seasons. We would see clearly the skeleton of unbreakable air that unites all the Peninsular regions—a skeleton held in suspension over the rain, with the naked sensibility of a mollusk, swallowing in the smallest invasion from the outside world and emitting, unthreatened, the most ancient and complex substance of Spain.

DEEP SONG

I

You have gathered tonight in the salon of the Centro Artístico to hear my simple but sincere word, and I would like it to be luminous and profound enough to convince you of the marvelous artistic truth contained in the primitive Andalusian music called "deep song."[1]

The intellectuals and enthusiastic friends backing the idea of this festival are only sounding an alarm. Gentlemen, the musical soul of our people is in great danger! The artistic treasure of an entire race is passing into oblivion. Each day another leaf falls from the admirable tree of Andalusian lyrics, old men carry off to the grave priceless treasures of past generations, and a gross, stupid avalanche of cheap music clouds the delicious folk atmosphere of all Spain.

We are trying to do something worthy and patriotic, a labor of salvation, friendship, and love.

You have all heard of deep song and have some idea what it is, but to those of you who are unaware of its historical and artistic transcendence it almost certainly suggests immoral things, the tavern, rowdy parties, the café dance floor, ridiculous whining—in short, all that is "typically Spanish"!—and we must guard against this for the sake of Andalusia, our millennial spirit, and each of our own hearts.

It does not seem possible that the deepest, most moving songs of our mysterious soul should be maligned as debauched and dirty; that people should want to tie to the orgiast's guitar the thread that connects us to the impenetrable Orient, and dash the dark wine of the professional pimp on the most diamantine part of our song.

And so the time has come for musicians, poets, and Spanish artists to unite their voices in an instinct of preservation, in order to define and exalt the limpid beauty and suggestiveness of these songs.

To confuse the patriotic and artistic ideals of this festival with the lamentable vision of the cantaor with his little tap-stick and his vulgar wailing about cemeteries would show total ignorance and misunderstanding of what has been planned. On reading the announcement of this competition, every sensible man uninformed on the matter will ask, "What is deep song?"

Before going ahead we ought to make a special distinction between deep song and flamenco—an essential distinction based on their relative antiquity, structure, and spirit.

The name deep song is given to a group of Andalusian songs whose genuine, perfect prototype is the Gypsy siguiriya. From the siguiriya are derived other songs still sung by the people—polos, martinetes, carceleras, and soleares. The songs called malagueñas, granadinas, rondeñas, peteneras, etc., must be considered mere offshoots of the songs mentioned above, for they differ in both architecture and rhythm. These latter songs constitute the so-called flamenco repertory.

The great maestro Manuel de Falla, true glory of Spain and soul of this festival, believes that with their primitive style, the caña and the playera, which have all but disappeared, have the same composition as the siguiriya and its related forms, and that not too long ago they were its simple variants. Relatively recent texts make Falla suppose that during the first third of the nineteenth century the caña and the playera occupied the place we assign today to the siguiriya. Estébanez Calderón, in his lovely *Escenas andaluzas,* notes that the caña is the primitive trunk of the songs retaining their Arab and Moorish filiation, and observes, with characteristic perspicacity, that the word "caña" much resembles the word "gannia," which is Arabic for song.

The essential difference between deep song and flamenco is that the origins of the former must be sought in the primitive musical systems of India, in the very first manifestations of song, while flamenco, a consequence of deep song, did not acquire its definitive form until the eighteenth century.

Deep song is imbued with the mysterious color of primordial ages; flamenco is relatively modern song whose emotional interest fades before that of deep song. Local color versus spiritual color, that is the profound difference.

Like the primitive Indian musical systems, deep song is a stammer, a wavering emission of the voice, a marvelous buccal undulation that smashes the resonant cells of our tempered scale, eludes the cold, rigid staves of modern music, and makes the tightly closed flowers of the semitones blossom into a thousand petals.

Flamenco does not proceed by undulation but by leaps. Its rhythm is as sure as that of our own music, and it was born centuries after Guido of Arezzo had named the notes.

Deep song is akin to the trilling of birds, the song of the rooster, and the natural music of forest and fountain.

It is a very rare specimen of primitive song, the oldest in all Europe, and its notes carry the naked, spine-tingling emotion of the first Oriental races.

Maestro Falla, who has made a profound study of the subject, and on whose work I document my own, affirms that the Gypsy siguiriya is the prototype of deep song, and he roundly declares that it is perhaps the only genre of song on our continent that has conserved in all its purity, both structurally and stylistically, the most important characteristics of the primitive song of Oriental peoples.

But even before I knew of the Maestro's opinion, the Gypsy siguiriya had always evoked (I am an incurable lyrist) an endless road, a road without crossroads, ending at the pulsing fountain of the child Poetry, the road where the first bird died and the first arrow grew rusty.

The Gypsy siguiriya begins with a terrible scream that divides the landscape into two ideal hemispheres. It is the scream of dead generations, a poignant elegy for lost centuries, the pathetic evocation of love under other moons and other winds.

Then the melodic phrase begins to pry open the mystery of the tones and remove the precious stone of the sob, a resonant tear on the river of the voice. No Andalusian can help but shudder on hearing that scream. No regional song has comparable poetic greatness; seldom—very seldom—has the human spirit been able to create works of that sort.

Do not think that the siguiriya and its variants are simply songs transplanted from the Orient to the West. No. "It is more a matter of grafting," Falla writes, "or, better said, of coinciding sources which certainly were not revealed all of a sudden, but grew from accumulated secular, historical events on our Peninsula. Thus it is that the song of Andalusia, though essentially like that of a people geographically remote from us, possesses its own intimate, unmistakable national character."

II

The historical events Falla says have influenced our songs are these: the Spanish Church's adoption of Byzantine liturgical chant, the Saracen invasion, and the arrival in Spain of numerous bands of Gypsies. These are the mysterious roving folk who gave deep song its final form.

The Gypsy influence is shown by the term "Gypsy siguiriya" and by the extraordinary number of Gypsy words in the texts of the songs.

Not that this chant is purely Gypsy: the Gypsies live all over Europe, and in all regions of the Peninsula, but these songs are cultivated only by our Andalusian ones.

It is a purely Andalusian chant, which was budding in this region even before the Gypsies came.

The Maestro notes these essential similarities between deep song and certain extant songs of India: "Enharmonic modulation, melody that is usually restricted to the compass of a sixth, and the reiterative, almost obsessive use of one same note, a procedure proper to certain formulas of incantation, including recited ones we might call prehistoric and which have made some people suppose that song is older than language."

In this way, deep song, especially the siguiriya, sometimes seems like sung prose, destroying all sense of metric rhythm, though in fact its literary texts are assonant tercets or quatrains.

According to Falla:

"Although Gypsy melody is rich in ornamental turns, in it, as in the primitive Oriental songs, they are used only at certain moments, like expansions or sudden gusts of expression suggested by the emotive strength of the poem, and we must think of them more as ample vocal inflections than as ornamental turns, though they resemble the latter when translated into the geometric intervals of the tempered scale."

One can say for sure that in deep song, as in the songs from the heart of Asia, the musical gamut is a direct consequence of what we might call the oral gamut.

Many authors suppose that word and song were once the same thing, and Louis Lucas, in his *Acoustique Nouvelle* (Paris, 1840) says, while discussing the excellence of the enharmonic genre, "It is the first which appears in Nature, through the imitation of birdsong, the cries of animals, and the infinite sounds of matter."

Hugo Riemann, in his *Musical Aesthetics* [*sic*], affirms that the song of birds is close to being true music, and cannot be treated differently than the song of men, insofar as both are the expression of sensibilities.

The great maestro Felipe Pedrell, one of the first Spaniards to study folklore scientifically, writes in his magnificent *Cancionero popular español:* "Musical orientalism persists in various popular Spanish songs and is deeply rooted in our nation owing to the influence of the ancient Byzantine civilization on the ritual formulas of the Spanish Church. This influence persisted from the conversion of our country to Christianity until the eleventh century, when the Roman liturgy . . . was introduced.

Falla adds to what his old teacher has said, ascertaining the elements of the Byzantine liturgical chant that are found in the siguiriya—the tonal modes of primitive systems (not to be confused with the so-called Greek modes), their inherent enharmonism, and the melodic line's lack of metric rhythm. "These properties also characterize certain Andalusian songs which appeared much later than the Spanish Church's adoption of Byzantine liturgical music, and which are closely akin to the music that in Morocco, Algiers, and Tunis is still called (this will move all true Granadans) 'music of the Moors of Granada.' "

But to return to the analysis of the siguiriya, Falla, with his solid musical knowledge and exquisite intuition, has found in it "certain forms and characteristics related neither to sacred chant nor to the 'music of the Moors of Granada.' " That is, having searched the strange melody of deep song, Falla has found an extraordinary agglutinative Gypsy element. He accepts the historical thesis that gives the Gypsies an Indic origin; and that thesis seems to agree marvelously with his fascinating research.

According to the thesis, in the year 1400 the Gypsies, pursued by the hundred thousand horsemen of the great Tamerlane, fled from India.

Twenty years later these tribes appeared in different European cities and entered Spain with the Saracen armies then periodically arriving (from Egypt and Arabia) on our coasts.

On arriving in Andalusia, the Gypsies combined ancient, indigenous elements with what they themselves brought, and gave what we now call deep song its definitive form.

So it is to them we owe the creation of these songs, soul of our soul.

We owe the Gypsies the building of these lyrical channels through which all the pain, all the ritual gestures of the race can escape.

And these are the songs, gentlemen, that for over fifty years Spaniards have tried to confine to fetid taverns and brothels. The terrible, doubting epoch of Grilo,[2] of the Spanish zarzuela and of historical painting, is to blame. While Russia burned with love for folklore, the one source, as Robert Schumann once said, of all true, characteristic art, and while the gilded wave of Impressionism trembled in France, in Spain, a country almost unique in her tradition of popular beauty, the guitar and deep song were scorned.

The prejudice has become so widespread that we must now cry out to defend songs so pure and true.

That is the way the spiritual youth of Spain understands it.

Cultivated since time immemorial, the deep song's profound psalmody has moved every illustrious traveler who ever ventured across our strange, varied landscapes. From the peaks of the Sierra Nevada to the thirsty olive groves of Córdoba, from the Sierra de Cazorla to the joyful mouth of the Guadalquivir, deep song has traversed and defined our unique, complicated land of Andalusia.

From when Jovellanos called attention to the lovely incoherent danza prima of Asturias until the time of the formidable Menéndez Pelayo, much progress was made in understanding folklore. Isolated artists, minor poets studied folklore from different points of view until they were able to begin the patriotic task of collecting poems and songs. Evidences of this are the *Songbook of Burgos* by Federico Olmeda, the *Songbook of Salamanca* by Dámaso Ledesma, and Eduardo Martínez Torner's *Asturian Songbook,* all generously subsidized by the respective provincial governments.

But the way we can really gauge the importance of deep song is by its almost decisive influence on the formation of the modern Russian school, and by the high esteem of the French composer Claude Debussy, that lyrical argonaut, discoverer of a new musical world.

In 1847 Mikhail Ivanovich Glinka came to Granada. He had been in Berlin studying composition with Siegfried Dehn and had observed the musical patriotism of Weber struggling against the pernicious influence of the Italian composers in Germany. Glinka was deeply impressed with the songs of Russia, immense Russia, and he dreamed of a natural music, a national music, that would convey some feeling of her grandeur.

The visit to our city by the father and founder of the Slavic-Orientalist school is more than curious. He made friends with a celebrated guitarist of those days, Francisco Rodríguez Murciano; for hours on end he listened to him play the variations and accompaniments to our songs. Amid the eternal rhythm of Granada's waters Glinka conceived the magnificent idea of creating his school and the courage to use the whole-tone scale for the first time.

When he returned to his people he announced the good news and explained the peculiarities of our songs, which he studied and used in his music.

Music changes direction! At last the composer has found its true source!

Glinka's friends and disciples turn to folklore and seek structures for their creations not only in Russia but in the south of Spain.

Proofs of this are Glinka's *Souvenirs d'une nuit d'été à Madrid* and parts of the *Scheherezade* and *Capriccio Espagnol* of Nicolai Rimsky-Korsakov, pieces you know.

Imagine the influence, all the way from Granada to Moscow, of the sad modulations and sober orientalism of our deep song, as the mysterious bells of the Kremlin catch the melancholy of the bell of the Vela.[3]

At the Spanish Pavilion of the great Paris Exhibition of 1900, a group of Gypsies sang deep song in all its purity. They startled the whole city, but especially a young musician who was then engaged in the fight all we young artists must carry on, the fight for what is new and unforeseen, the treasure hunt, in the sea of thought, for inviolate emotion.

Day after day that young man went to hear the Andalusian cantaores, and he whose soul was wide open to the four winds of the spirit was soon made pregnant by the ancient Orient of our melodies. He was Claude Debussy.

Later he would define new theories and become the very summit of European music.

Sure enough, from his compositions rise the subtlest evocations of Spain, above all of Granada, a city he knew for what it really is: paradise.

Claude Debussy, composer of fragrance and of iridescence, reaches his highest creative pitch in the poem *Iberia,* a truly genial work in which Andalusian perfumes and essences dreamily float.

But where he reveals precisely how much he was influenced by deep song is in the marvelous prelude titled *La Puerta del Vino* and in the vague, tender *Soirée en Grenade,* where, I think, one can find all the emotional themes of the Granadan night, the blue remoteness of the "vega," the Sierra greeting the tremulous Mediterranean, the enormous barbs of the clouds sunk into the distance, the admirable rubato of the city, the hallucinating play of its underground waters.

And the most remarkable thing about all this is that Debussy, though he seriously studied our song, never saw Granada.

It is a stupendous case of artistic divination, of profound and brilliant intuition, which I mention in praise of the great composer and to the honor of our people. It reminds me of the great mystic Swedenborg when he saw, all the way from London, the burning of Stockholm, and of the profound prophecies of the saints of antiquity.

In Spain deep song has undeniably influenced all the best composers, from Albéniz through Granados to Falla. Felipe Pedrell had already used popular songs in his magnificent opera *La Celestina* (to our shame never performed in Spain) and had showed where we were headed. But the master stroke was left to Isaac Albéniz, who used the lyrical depths of Andalusian song in his work. Years later Manuel de Falla fills his music with our motifs, beautiful and pure in their faraway, spectral form. The latest generation of Spanish composers, like Adolfo Salazar, Roberto Gerhard, Federico Mompou, and our own Angel Barrios, enthusiastic organizers of this festival, are training their sight on the pure, revivifying font of deep song and on the delightful songs of Granada, songs that might well be called Castilian-Andalusian.

Notice, gentlemen, the transcendence of deep song, and how rightly our people called it "deep." It is truly deep, deeper than all the wells and seas that surround the world, much deeper than the present heart that creates it or the voice that sings it, because it is almost infinite. It comes from remote races and crosses the graveyard of the years and the fronds of parched winds. It comes from the first sob and the first kiss.

One of the marvels of deep song, apart from the melodies, is the poems.

All us poets who to some degree are concerned with pruning and caring for the overluxuriant lyric tree left to us by the Romantics and post-Romantics are astonished by these poems.

The finest degrees of Sorrow and Pain, in the service of the purest, most exact expression, pulse through the tercets and quatrains of the siguiriya and its derivatives.

There is nothing, absolutely nothing in Spain, to equal the siguiriya's style, atmosphere, and emotional rightness.

The metaphors that people the Andalusian songbook are almost always within the siguiriya's orbit. The spiritual members of its verses are uniformly excellent; they seize our hearts and hold them fast.

It is wondrous and strange how in just three or four lines the anonymous popular poet can condense all the highest emotional moments in human life. There are songs where the lyric tremor reaches a point inaccessible to any but a few poets:

Cerco tiene la luna,	The moon has a halo,
mi amor ha muerto.	my love has died.

There is much more mystery in those two lines than in all the plays of Maeterlinck. Simple, genuine mystery, clean and sound, without gloomy forests or rudderless ships. It is the living, eternal enigma of death:

Cerco tiene la luna,
mi amor ha muerto.

Whether they come from the heart of the Sierra, the orange groves of Seville, or from harmonious Mediterranean shores, the songs have common roots: love and death. But love and death as seen by the Sibyl, that Oriental personage, the true sphinx of Andalusia.[4]

At the bottom of all these poems lurks a terrible question that has no answer. Our people cross their arms in prayer, look at the stars, and wait uselessly for a sign of salvation. The gesture is pathetic but true. And the poem either poses a deep emotional question that cannot be answered, or solves it with death, which is the question of questions.

Most of Andalusia's popular poems, except for many born in Seville, possess those characteristics. We are a sad, static people.

As Ivan Turgenev saw his countrymen (Russian blood and marrow turned to sphinx), so do I see many poems of our regional folk poetry. Oh sphinx of the Andalusias!

A mi puerta has de llamar,	You will knock at my door.
no te he de salir a abrir	I will never get up to answer.
y me has de sentir llorar.	You will have to hear me cry.

Asleep behind an impenetrable veil, those lines await a passing Oedipus to awaken and decipher them, and then return them to silence.

One of the most notable characteristics of the poems of deep song is their almost complete lack of a restrained, middle tone.

In the songs of Asturias, as in those of Castile, Catalonia, the Basque country, and Galicia, there is a certain emotional balance, a lyrical meditation that lends itself to the expression of simple states of mind and naïve feeling almost entirely missing from the Andalusian songs.

Seldom do we Andalusians notice the "middle tone." An Andalusian either shouts at the stars or kisses the red dust of the road. The middle tone does not exist for him; he sleeps right through it. And when he uses it, once in a great while, all he says is:[5]

A mí se me importa poco	It doesn't matter to *me*
que un pajaro en la "alamea"	if a bird in the poplar grove
se pase un árbol a otro.	has skipped from tree to tree.

And even this song is related to Asturian songs in sentiment, if not in architecture. So then, emotiveness is the most striking characteristic of our deep song.

That is why, though many of the songs of our Peninsula can make us see the landscapes where they are sung, deep song sings like a nightingale without eyes. It sings blind, for both its words and its ancient tunes are best set in the night, the blue night of our countryside.

The capacity of many Spanish popular songs for plastic evocation deprives them of deep song's intimacy and profundity.

Here is one Asturian song (among a thousand others) that will serve as a fine example of this sort of "evocation":

Ay de mí, perdí el camino	Ah, I have lost the road
en esta triste montaña,	on this sad mountain.
ay de mí, perdí el camino.	Ah, I have lost the road.
Déẍame meté'l rebañu,	Let me bring the sheep
por Dios, en la to cabaña.	for God's sake into your cabin;
Entre la espesa nublina	in the thick clouds
¡ay de mí, perdí el camino!,	I lost the road.
déẍame pasar la noche	Let me spend the night
en la cabaña contigo.	in the cabin with you.
Perdí el camino	I lost the road
entre la niebla del monte,	in the mountain mist.
¡ay de mí, perdí el camino!	Ah, I have lost the road.

It is so marvelous, this evocation of a mountain, with the wind moving the pine trees; so exact the sensation of the road climbing to the peaks where the snow is asleep; so true the sight of the mist coming up from the abyss to blur the moist rocks in innumerable shades of gray—it is so marvelous that one forgets all about the "honest shepherd" who, like a little boy, asks shelter of the poem's unknown shepherd girl. "One forgets the very essence of the poem." The melody of this song, with its monotonous green-gray rhythm of misty landscapes, is extraordinarily suggestive, plastically.

In contrast, deep song always sings in the night. It knows neither morning nor evening, mountains nor plains. It has nothing but the night, a wide night steeped in stars. Nothing else matters.

It is song without landscape, withdrawn into itself and terrible in the dark. Deep song shoots its arrows of gold right into our heart. In the dark it is a terrifying blue archer whose quiver is never empty.

The questions everybody asks—who made these poems? what anonymous poet tossed them onto the rude popular stage?—these questions really cannot be answered.

In his book *Les origines de la poésie lyrique en France,* Jeanroy writes that popular art is not only impersonal, vague, unconscious creation; it includes also the "personal" creations that the people adapt to their own sensibility. Jeanroy is partly correct, but one need not be very perceptive to discover such personal creations in hiding, however savage the colors that camouflage them. Our people sing poems of Melchor de Palau, of Salvador Rueda, of Ventura Ruiz Aguilera, of Manuel Machado and others, but what a difference between the verse of these poets and the poems the people created themselves! It is the difference between a paper rose and a natural one! The poets who compose "popular" songs cloud the clear lymph of the true heart. How one notices, in their poems, the confident, ugly rhythm of the man who knows grammar!

Nothing but the quintessence and this or that trill for its coloristic effect ought to be drawn straight from the people. We should never want to copy their ineffable modulations; we can do nothing but blur them. Simply because of education.

The true poems of deep song belong to no one—they float in the wind like golden thistledown, and each generation dresses them in a different color and passes them on to the next.

They are fastened to an ideal weathervane changing direction in the wind of Time.

They are born, well, just because. They are one more tree in the landscape, one more spring in the poplar grove.

Woman, heart of the world and immortal keeper of "the rose, the lyre, and the harmonious science" looms on the infinite horizons of these poems. The woman of deep song is called Pain.

It is admirable how sentiment begins to take shape in these lyrical constructions and quicken into an almost material thing. This is the case with Pain.

In these poems Pain is made flesh, takes human form, and shows her profile: she is a dark woman wanting to catch birds in nets of wind.

All of the poems of deep song are magnificently pantheistic; they consult the wind, the earth, the sea, the moon, and things as simple as a violet, a rosemary, a bird. All exterior objects assume their own striking personalities and even play active roles in the lyrical action:

[1]

En mitá der "má" había una piedra y se sentaba mi compañerita a contarle sus penas.	Out in the sea was a stone, and my girl sat down to tell it her pains.
Tan solamente a la Tierra le cuento lo que me pasa, porque en el mundo no encuentro persona e mi confianza.	Only to the Earth do I tell my troubles, for there is no one in the world whom I can trust.
Todas las mañanas voy a preguntarle al romero si el mal de amor tiene cura porque yo me estoy muriendo.	Every morning I go to ask the rosemary if love's disease can be cured, for I am dying.

With deep spiritual feeling, the Andalusian entrusts Nature with his whole intimate treasure, completely confident of being heard.

One feature of deep song, one admirable poetic reality, is the strange way the wind materializes in many of the songs.

The wind is a character who emerges in the ultimate, most emotional moments. He comes into sight like a giant absorbed in pulling down stars and scattering nebulae; and in no popular poetry but ours have I heard him speak and console:

[2]

Subí a la muralla me respondió el viento: ¿para que tantos suspiritos si ya no hay remedio?	I climbed up the wall. The wind answered me, "why so many sighs, if it is already too late?"
El aire lloró al ver las "duquitas" tan grandes e mi corazón.	The breeze wept when he saw the deep wounds in my heart.
Yo me enamoré del aire, del aire de una mujer, como la mujer es aire, en el aire me quedé	I fell in love with the air, the air of a woman, and since a woman is air, in the air I stayed.
Tengo celos del aire que da en tu cara, si el aire fuera hombre yo le matara.	I am jealous of the breeze that touches your face. If the breeze were a man, I would kill him.
Yo no le temo a remar que yo remar remaría. Yo solo temo al viento que sale de tu bahía.	I'm not afraid to row. If I wanted to row I'd do it. I'm just afraid of the wind that comes out of your bay.

This is a delicious peculiarity of these poems, poems tangled in the immobile helix of the mariner's wind chart.

Another very special theme, one repeated in most of these songs, is weeping.

In the Gypsy siguiriya, perfect poem of tears, the melody cries, and so does the poetry. There are bells lost in the deep, windows open to the dawn:

De noche me sargo ar patio y me jarto de llorá, en ver que te quiero tanto y tú no me quieres ná.	At night I go to the courtyard and cry my fill of tears to see I love you so much and you don't love me at all.

Llorar, llorar, ojos míos,	Cry, keep crying, eyes,
llorar si tenéis por que,	cry if you have cause.
que no es vergüenza en un hombre	It shouldn't shame a man
llorar por una mujer.	to cry over a woman.
Cuando me veas llorar	When you see me cry
no me quites el pañuelo,	leave me my handkerchief.
que mis penitas son grandes	My pains are so huge
y llorando me consuelo.	that crying I feel better.

And this last one, very Andalusian and very Gypsy:[6]

Si mi corazón tuviera	If my heart had
birieritas e cristar,	windowpanes of glass
te asomaras y lo vieras	you would look in and see it
gotas de sangre llorar.	cry drops of blood.

These songs have an unmistakably popular air, and are in my judgment the ones best suited to the melancholy of deep song. Their sadness is so irresistible, their emotiveness so strong that they cause all true Andalusians to weep inside, with tears that wash the spirit and carry it away to the burning lemon grove of love.

Nothing can compare with the tenderness and delicacy of these songs, and I insist again that it is infamy to forget them or to prostitute them with base, sensual intention or gross caricature. But that only happens in cities. Fortunately for the virgin Poetry and for all poets, there are still sailors who sing at sea, women who rock their children to sleep in the shade of grapevines, and churlish shepherds on mountain paths. The passionate wind of poetry will throw fuel on the dying fire, livening its flames, and these people will continue to sing—the women in the shade of the vine, the shepherds on their bitter paths, the sailors on the fecund rhythm of the sea.

Just as very ancient Oriental elements are found in the music of the siguiriya and its daughter genres, so in many poems of deep song there is an affinity to the oldest Eastern verse.

When our songs reach the very extremes of pain and love they become the expressive sisters of the magnificent verses of Arabian and Persian poets.

The truth is that in the air of Córdoba and Granada one still finds gestures and lines of remote Arabia, and remembrances of lost cities still arise from the murky palimpsest of the Albaicín.

The same themes of sacrifice, undying love, and wine, expressed in the same spirit, appear in the works of mysterious Asiatic poets.

The Arabic poet Siraj-al-Warak says:

The turtledove that with her complaints
keeps me from sleep
has a breast that burns like mine,
alive with fire.

Ibn Sa'īd,[7] another Arabic poet, writes the same elegy that an Andalusian would have written, on the death of his mistress:

To console me my friends say
visit your mistress's tomb.
Has she a tomb, I answer,
other than in my breast?

But where the resemblance is most striking of all is in the sublime amorous ghazals of Hafiz, the national poet of Persia, who sang the wine, beautiful women, mysterious stones, and infinite blue night of Shiraz.

Since ancient times art has used wireless telegraphy and the little reflectors of the stars.

In his ghazals Hafiz shows various poetic obsessions, among them an exquisite obsession with tresses:

Even if she did not love me,
I would trade
the whole ball of the earth
for one hair from her tress.

And later he writes:

My heart has been ensnared
in your black tress since childhood.
Not until death
will such a wonderful bond be undone.

The same obsession with hair is found in many of our singular deep song poems, full of allusions to tresses preserved in reliquaries and the lock of hair on the forehead that provokes a whole tragedy. This specimen, one of many, demonstrates my point. It is a siguiriya.

Si acasito muero mira que	If I should happen to die,
te encargo	I order you,
que con las trenzas de tu pelo negro	tie up my hands
me ates las manos.	with the tress of your black hair.

There is nothing more profundly poetic than those three lines, with their sad, aristocratic eroticism.

When Hafiz takes up the theme of weeping he uses the same expressions as our popular poet, with the same spectral construction, based on the same sentiments:

I weep endlessly; you are gone.
But what use is all my longing
if the wind will not take my sighs
to your ears . . .

It is the same as:

Yo doy suspiros al aire,	I sigh into the wind
¡ay pobrecito de mí!	poor me!
y no los recoge nadie.	And nobody catches my sighs.

Hafiz says:

Since you stopped listening
to the echo of my voice,
my heart has been plunged in pain.
It sends jets of burning blood
to my eyes.

And our poet:

Cada vez que miro el sitio	Whenever I look at the place
donde te he solido hablar	where I used to talk to you,

comienzan mis pobres ojos	my poor eyes begin
gotas de sangre a llorar.	crying drops of blood.

Or this terrible poem, a siguiriya:

De aquellos quereres	I must not remember
no quiero acordarme,	that love;
porque llora mi corazoncito	my heart is crying
gotas de sangre.	blood drops.

In the twenty-seventh ghazal the man of Shiraz sings:

In the end my bones
will turn to dust in the grave,
but the soul will never be able
to lose such a strong love.

Which is exactly the same solution struck by countless poets of deep song: love is stronger than death.

It moved me deeply to read these Asiatic poems translated into Spanish by Don Gaspar María de Nava and published in Paris in 1838, for they immediately reminded me of our own "deepest" poems.

Then too, both our "siguiriyeros" and the Oriental poets praise wine. They praise the clear, relaxing wine that reminds one of girls' lips, happy wine, quite unlike the frightening Baudelairean stuff. I will cite one song (I think it is a martinete) which is sung by a character who tells us his Christian name and surname, a rare occurrence. I see all true Andalusian poets personified in him.

Yo me llamo Curro Pulla	They call me Curro Pulla
por la tierra y por el mar,	on land and on the sea.
y en la puerta de la tasca	I am the bottom stone in
la piedra fundamental.	the portal of the tavern.

In these songs of Curro Pulla wine is given its greatest eulogy. Like the marvelous Omar Khayyam, he knows that

My love will end,
my grief will end,

my tears will end,
and all will end.

Crowning himself with the roses of the moment, he gazes into a glass of nectar and sees a falling star. Like the magnificent bard of Nishapur he perceives life to be a chessboard.

Gentlemen, deep song, because of both its melody and its poems, is one of the strongest popular artistic creations in the world. In your hands is the task of preserving it and dignifying it, for the sake of Andalusia and her people.

Before I bring this poor, badly constructed lecture to a close, I want to remember the marvelous singers thanks to whom deep song has come down to our day.

The figure of the cantaor is found within two great lines, the arc of the sky on the outside, and on the inside the zigzag that wanders like a snake through his heart.

When the cantaor sings he is celebrating a solemn rite, as he rouses ancient essences from their sleep, wraps them in his voice, and flings them into the wind . . . He has a deeply religious sense of song.

Through these chanters the race releases its pain and its true history. They are simple mediums, the lyrical crest of our people.

They are strange but simple folk who sing hallucinated by a brilliant point trembling on the horizon.

The women have sung soleares, a melancholy, human genre within easy reach of the heart; but the men have preferred to cultivate the portentous Gypsy siguiriya, and almost all of them have been martyrs to an irresistible passion for deep song. The siguiriya is like a cautery that burns the heart, throat, and lips of those who speak it. One must be careful of the fire and sing at just the right moment.

I want to remember Romerillo, the spiritual "Loco Mateo," Antonia "la de San Roque," Anita "la de Ronda," Dolores la Parrala, and Juan Breva, who all sang soleares better than anyone else and called on the virgin Pain in the lemon groves of Málaga or beneath the maritime nights of Cadiz.

And I want to remember the masters of the siguiriya: Curro Pabla "el Curro," Manuel Molina, Manuel Torre, and the prodigious Silverio Franconetti, who sang the song of songs better than anyone and whose scream used to open into quivering cracks the moribund mercury of the mirrors.[8]

They were prodigious interpreters of the people's soul who destroyed their own hearts in storms of feeling. Almost all died of heart attacks; they exploded like enormous cicadas after populating our atmosphere with ideal rhythms . . .

Ladies and gentlemen, if you have ever been moved by the distant song that comes down the road; if your ripe hearts have ever been pinched by the white dove of Love; if you love the tradition that is strung (as beads are strung) upon the future; whether you study books or plow the earth—I respectfully appeal to all of you not to allow the precious living jewels of the race—the immense, thousand-year-old treasure that covers the spiritual surface of Andalusia—not to let that die. May you meditate, beneath this Granadan night, on the patriotic transcendence of the project a handful of Spanish artists are about to present.

PLAY AND THEORY OF THE DUENDE

LADIES AND GENTLEMEN:

From 1918, when I entered the Residencia de Estudiantes de Madrid, until 1928, when I finished my studies in Philosophy and Letters and left, I attended, in that elegant room where the old Spanish aristocracy used to do penance for its frivolous seaside vacations in France, around one thousand lectures.[1]

Hungry for air and for sunlight, I used to grow so bored as to feel myself covered by a light film of ash about to turn into sneezing powder.

And that is why I promise never to let the terrible botfly of boredom into *this* room, stringing your heads together on the fine thread of sleep and putting tiny pins and needles in your eyes.

As simply as possible, in the register of my poetic voice that has neither the glow of woodwinds nor bends of hemlocks, nor sheep who suddenly turn into knives of irony, I shall try to give you a simple lesson in the hidden spirit of disconsolate Spain.[2]

Whoever finds himself on the bull's hide stretched between the Júcar, Guadalfeo, Sil, and Pisuerga rivers—not to mention the great streams that meet the tawny waves churned by the Plata—often hears people say, "This has much duende." Manuel Torre, great artist of the Andalusian people,[3] once told a singer, "You have a voice, you know the styles, but you will never triumph, because you have no duende."

All over Andalusia, from the rock of Jaén to the whorled shell of

Cádiz, the people speak constantly of the "duende," and identify it accurately and instinctively whenever it appears. The marvelous singer El Lebrijano, creator of the debla, used to say, "On days when I sing with duende, no one can touch me." The old Gypsy dancer La Malena once heard Brailowsky play a fragment of Bach and exclaimed, "Olé! That has duende!" but was bored by Gluck, Brahms, and Darius Milhaud. Manuel Torre, who had more culture in the blood than any man I have ever known, pronounced this splendid sentence on hearing Falla play his own *Nocturno del Generalife:* "All that has black sounds has duende." And there is no greater truth.

These black sounds are the mystery, the roots fastened in the mire that we all know and all ignore, the mire that gives us the very substance of art. "Black sounds," said that man of the Spanish people, concurring with Goethe, who defined the duende while speaking of Paganini: "A mysterious power which everyone senses and no philosopher explains."[4]

The duende, then, is a power, not a work; it is a struggle, not a thought. I have heard an old maestro of the guitar say, "The duende is not in the throat; the duende climbs up inside you, from the soles of the feet." Meaning this: it is not a question of ability, but of true, living style, of blood, of the most ancient culture, of spontaneous creation.

This "mysterious power which everyone senses and no philosopher explains" is, in sum, the spirit of the earth, the same duende that scorched the heart of Nietzsche, who looked for its external forms on the Rialto Bridge and in the music of Bizet, without ever finding it and without knowing that the duende he was pursuing had leaped straight from the Greek mysteries to the dancers of Cádiz or the beheaded, Dionysian scream of Silverio's siguiriya.[5]

But I do not want anyone to confuse the duende with the theological demon of doubt at whom Luther, with bacchic feeling, hurled a poet of ink in [Eisenach], nor with the destructive and rather stupid Catholic devil who disguises himself as a bitch to get into convents, nor with the talking monkey carried by Cervantes' Malgesi in his *Comedy of Jealousy and the Forest of Ardenia.*

No. The duende I am talking about is the dark, shuddering descendant of the happy marble-and-salt demon of Socrates, whom he angrily scratched on the day Socrates swallowed the hemlock, and of that melancholy demon of Descartes, a demon who was small as a green almond and who sickened of circles and lines and escaped down the canals to listen to the songs of blurry sailors.

Every man and every artist, whether he is Nietzsche or Cézanne, climbs each step in the tower of his perfection by fighting his duende, not his angel, as has been said, nor his muse. This distinction is fundamental, at the very root of the work.

The angel guides and gives like Saint Raphael, defends and avoids like Saint Michael, announces and forewarns like Saint Gabriel.

The angel dazzles, but he flies high over a man's head, shedding his grace, and the man effortlessly realizes his work or his charm or his dance. The angel on the road to Damascus and the one that came through the crack of the little balcony at Assisi, and the one who tracked Heinrich Suso are all *ordering,* and it is no use resisting their lights, for they beat their steel wings in an atmosphere of predestination.

The muse dictates and sometimes prompts. She can do relatively little, for she is distant and so tired (I saw her twice) that one would have to give her half a heart of marble. Poets who have muses hear voices and do not know where they are coming from. They come from the muse that encourages them and sometimes snacks on them, as happened to Apollinaire, a great poet destroyed by the horrible muse the divine, angelic Rousseau painted him with. The muse awakens the intelligence, bringing a landscape of columns and a false taste of laurels. But intelligence is often the enemy of poetry, because it limits too much, and it elevates the poet to a sharp-edged throne where he forgets that ants could eat him or that a great arsenic lobster could fall on his head—things against which the muses that live in monocles and in the lukewarm lacquered roses of tiny salons are quite helpless.

The muse and angel come from without; the angel gives lights, and the muse gives forms (Hesiod learned from her). Loaf of gold or tunic fold: the poet receives norms in his bosk of laurels. But one must awaken the duende in the remotest mansions of the blood.

And reject the angel, and give the muse a kick in the seat of the pants, and conquer our fear of the smile of violets exhaled by eighteenth-century poetry and of the great telescope in whose lens the muse, sickened by limits, is sleeping.

The true fight is with the duende.

We know the roads where we can search for God, from the barbarous way of the hermit to the subtle one of the mystic. With a tower like Saint Theresa or with the three ways of Saint John of the Cross. And though we may have to cry out in the voice of Isaiah, "Truly thou art a hidden God," in the end God sends each seeker his first fiery thorns.

But there are neither maps nor disciplines to help us find the duende. We only know that he burns the blood like a poultice of broken glass, that he exhausts, that he rejects all the sweet geometry we have learned, that he smashes styles and makes Goya (master of the grays, silvers, and pinks of the best English painting) work with his fists and knees in horrible bitumins. He strips Mossèn Cinto Verdaguer in the cold of the Pyrenees, or takes Jorge Manrique to watch for death in the wasteland of Ocaña, or dresses Rimbaud's delicate body in the green suit of a saltimbanque, or puts the eyes of a dead fish on the Comte de Lautréamont in the early morning of the boulevard.

The great artists of the south of Spain, whether Gypsy or flamenco, whether they sing, dance, or play, know that no emotion is possible unless the duende comes. They may be able to fool people into thinking they have duende—authors and painters and literary fashionmongers do so every day—but we have only to pay a little attention and not surrender to our own indifference in order to discover their fraud and chase away their clumsy artifice.

The Andalusian singer Pastora Pavón, "La Niña de los Peines," dark Hispanic genius whose powers of fantasy are equal to those of Goya or Rafael el Gallo, was once singing in a little tavern in Cádiz. For a while she played with her voice of shadow, of beaten tin, her moss-covered voice, braiding it into her hair or soaking it in wine or letting it wander away to the farthest, darkest bramble patches. No use. Nothing. The audience remained silent.

In the same room was Ignacio Espeleta, handsome as a Roman tortoise, who had once been asked, "How come you don't work?" and had answered, with a smile worthy of Argantonius, "Work? I'm from Cádiz!" And there was Hot Elvira, aristocrat, Sevillian whore, direct descendant of Soledad Vargas, who in 1930 refused to marry a Rothschild because he was not of equal blood. And the Floridas, whom the people take to be butchers but who are really millennial priests who still sacrifice bulls to Geryon. And in one corner sat the formidable bull rancher Don Pablo Murube, with the air of a Cretan mask. When Pastora Pavón finished singing there was total silence, until a tiny man, one of those dancing manikins that rise suddenly out of brandy bottles, sarcastically murmured "¡Viva Paris!" as if to say: "Here we care nothing about ability, technique, skill. Here we are after something else."

As though crazy, torn like a medieval weeper, La Niña de los Peines got to her feet, tossed off a big glass of firewater and began to sing with a scorched throat, without voice, without breath or color, but with duende. She was able to kill all the scaffolding of the song and leave way for a furious, enslaving duende, friend of sand winds, who made the listeners rip their clothes with the same rhythm as do the blacks of the Antilles when, in the "lucumí" rite, they huddle in heaps before the statue of Santa Bárbara.

La Niña de los Peines had to tear her voice because she knew she had an exquisite audience, one which demanded not forms but the marrow of forms, pure music with a body so lean it could stay in the air. She had to rob herself of skill and security, send away her muse and become helpless, that her duende might come and deign to fight her hand to hand. And how she sang! Her voice was no longer playing, it was a jet of blood worthy of her pain and her sincerity, and it opened like a ten-fingered hand around the nailed but stormy feet of a Christ by Juan de Juni.

The duende's arrival always means a radical change in forms. It brings to old planes unknown feelings of freshness, with the quality of something newly created, like a miracle, and it produces an almost religious enthusiasm.

In all Arabic music, whether dance, song, or elegy, the duende's arrival is greeted with energetic cries of Allah! Allah!, which is so close to the Olé of the bullfight that who knows if it is not the same thing? And in all the songs of the south of Spain the duende is greeted with sincere cries of ¡Viva Dios!—deep and tender human cry of communication with God through the five senses, thanks to the duende, who shakes the body and voice of the dancer. It is a real and poetic evasion of this world, as pure as that of the strange seventeenth-century poet Pedro Soto de Rojas with his seven gardens, or that of John Climacus with his tremulous ladder of lamentation.

Naturally, when this evasion succeeds, everyone feels its effects, both the initiate, who sees that style has conquered a poor material, and the unenlightened, who feel some sort of authentic emotion. Years ago, an eighty-year-old woman won first prize at a dance contest in Jerez de la Frontera. She was competing against beautiful women and young girls with waists supple as water, but all she did was raise her arms, throw back her head, and stamp her foot on the floor. In that gathering of muses and angels, beautiful forms and beautiful smiles, who could have won but her moribund duende, sweeping the ground with its wings of rusty knives.[6]

All arts are capable of duende, but where it finds greatest range, naturally, is in music, dance, and spoken poetry, for these arts require a living body to interpret them, being forms that are born, die, and open their contours against an exact present.

Often the duende of the composer passes into the duende of the interpreter, and at other times, when a composer or poet is no such thing, the interpreter's duende—this is interesting—creates a new marvel that looks like, but is not, the primitive form. This was the case of the duende-ridden Eleanora Duse, who looked for plays that had failed so she could make them triumph thanks to her own inventions, and the case of Paganini, as explained by Goethe, who made one hear deep melodies in vulgar trifles, and the case of a delightful little girl I saw in Port St. Marys singing and dancing that horrible, corny Italian song "O Marí!" with such rhythms, silences, and intention that she turned the Neopolitan gewgaw into a hard serpent of raised gold. All three of these people had found something new and totally unprecedented that could give lifeblood and art to bodies devoid of expressiveness.

Every art and in fact every country is capable of duende, angel, and muse. And just as Germany has, with few exceptions, muse, and Italy shall always have angel, so in all ages Spain is moved by the duende, for it is a country of ancient music and dance where the duende squeezes the lemons of dawn—a country of death. A country open to death.

Everywhere else, death is an end. Death comes, and they draw the curtains. Not in Spain. In Spain they open them. Many Spaniards live indoors until the day they die and are taken out into the sunlight. A dead man in Spain is more alive as a dead man than any place else in the world. His profile wounds like the edge of a barber's razor. The joke about death and its silent contemplation are familiar to every Spaniard. From Quevedo's *Dream of the Skulls* to Valdés Leal's *Putrescent Archbishop,* from seventeenth-century Marbella who says, while dying of childbirth in the middle of the road:[7]

La sangre de mis entrañas	The blood of my insides
cubriendo el caballo está.	is covering the horse.
Las patas de tu caballo	The horse's hoofs
echan fuego de alquitrán . . .	throw off black fire.

to the recent youth of Salamanca who is killed by a bull and moans:[8]

Amigos, que yo me muero; | Friends, I am dying.
amigos, yo estoy muy malo. | Friends, it is pretty bad.
Tres pañuelos tengo dentro | Three handkerchiefs in me
y este que meto son cuatro . . . | and this makes a fourth . . .

stretches a balustrade of saltpeter flowers[9] where the Spanish people go to contemplate death. On one side, the more rugged one, are the verses of Jeremiah, and on the other, more lyrical side is a fragrant cypress. But throughout the country, everything finds its final, metallic value in death.

The hut and the cart wheel and the razor and the prickly beards of the shepherds and the peeled moon and the fly and moist pantry shelves and torn-down buildings and lace-covered saints and lime and the wounding line of eaves and miradors possess, in Spain, fine weeds of death, the allusions and murmurings (perceptible to any alert spirit) that fill our memory with the stale air of our own passage. It is no accident that Spanish art is tied to the land, all thistles and terminal stones. The lamentation of Pleberio,[10] the dances of Maestro Josef María de Valdivielso, are not isolated examples, and it is hardly a matter of chance that this beloved Spanish ballad stands apart from all others in Europe:[11]

—Si tú eres mi linda amiga, | If you are my pretty friend
¿cómo no me miras, di? | why don't you look at me?
—Ojos con que te miraba | The eyes I looked at you with
a la sombra se los di. | I have given to the dark.
—Si tú eres mi linda amiga, | If you are my pretty friend,
¿cómo no me besas, di? | why don't you kiss me?
—Labios con que te besaba | The lips I kissed you with
a la tierra se los di. | I have given to the earth.
—Si tú eres mi linda amiga, | If you are my pretty friend
¿cómo no me abrazas, di? | why don't you hold me tight?
—Brazos con que te abrazaba, | The arms that I hugged you with
de gusanos los cubrí. | I have covered with worms.

Nor is it strange that this song is heard at the very dawn of our lyric poetry:[12]

Dentro del vergel | In the garden
moriré, | I will die.
dentro del rosal | In the rosebush

matar me han.	they will kill me.
Yo me iba, mi madre,	I was going, Mother,
las rosas coger,	to pick roses,
hallara la muerte	to find death
dentro del vergel.	in the garden.
Yo me iba, madre,	I was going, Mother,
las rosas cortar,	to cut roses,
hallara la muerte	to find death
dentro del rosal.	in the rosebush.
Dentro del vergel	In the garden
moriré,	I will die.
dentro del rosal	In the rosebush
matar me han.	they will kill me.

The moon-frozen heads that Zurbarán painted, the butter yellow and lightning yellow of El Greco, the narrative of Father Sigüenza, the whole work of Goya, the apse of the church of the Escorial, all polychromed sculpture, the crypt of the house of the Duke of Osuna, the "Death with a guitar" in the Chapel of the Benaventes at Medina de Rioseco—all these mean the same, culturally, as the processions of San Andrés de Teixido, where the dead play a role,[13] the dirges sung by Asturian women with flame-filled torches in the November night,[14] the chant and dance of the Sibyl in the cathedrals of Mallorca and Toledo, the dark "In Recort" of Tortosa,[15] and the innumerable rites of Good Friday which, along with the supremely civilized festival of the bullfight, are the popular triumph of Spanish death. In all the world, only Mexico can take my country's hand.

When the muse sees death arrive, she closes the door or raises a plinth or promenades an urn and writes an epitaph with waxen hand, but soon she is watering her laurel again in a silence that wavers between two breezes. Beneath the broken arch of the ode, she joins with funereal feeling the limpid flowers of fifteenth-century Italian painters, and asks Lucretius' trusty rooster to frighten away unforeseen shades.

When the angel sees death come, he flies in slow circles and weaves, from tears of narcissus and ice, the elegy we have seen tremble in the hands of Keats, Villasandino, Herrera, Bécquer, and Juan Ramón Jiménez. But how it horrifies him to feel even the tiniest spider on his tender, rosy foot!

And the duende? The duende does not come at all unless he sees that death is possible. The duende must know beforehand that he can serenade death's house and rock those branches we all wear, branches that do not have, will never have, any consolation.

With idea, sound, or gesture, the duende enjoys fighting the creator on the very rim of the well. Angel and muse escape with violin and compass; the duende wounds. In the healing of that wound, which never closes, lies the invented, strange qualities of a man's work.

The magical property of a poem is to remain possessed by duende that can baptize in dark water all who look at it, for with duende it is easier to love and understand, and one can be *sure* of being loved and understood. In poetry this struggle for expression and the communication of expression is sometimes fatal.

Think of the case of Saint Theresa, that supremely "flamenco" woman who was so filled with duende. "Flamenco" not because she caught a bull and gave it three magnificent passes (which she did!) and not because she thought herself very lovely in the presence of Fray Juan de Miseria, nor because she slapped the papal nuncio, but because she was one of the few creatures whose duende—not angel, for the angel never attacks—pierced her with a dart and wanted to kill her for having stolen his deepest secret, the subtle bridge that unites the fives senses with the raw wound, that living cloud, that stormy ocean of Love freed from Time.

Most valiant conqueror of the duende, the very opposite of Philip of Austria, who pined after the muse and angel in theology and was finally imprisoned by a duende of freezing ardor in the palace of the Escorial, where geometry borders on dream and the duende wears the mask of the muse to the eternal punishment of that great king.

We have said that the duende loves the rim of the wound, and that he draws near places where forms fuse together into a yearning superior to their visible expression.

In Spain, as among the peoples of the Orient, where the dance is religious expression, the duende has unlimited range over the bodies of the dancers of Cádiz, praised by Martial, over the breasts of singers, praised by Juvenal, and in the liturgy of the bulls, an authentic religious drama where, as in the Mass, a God is sacrificed to and adored.

It seems as if all the duende of the classical world has crowded into this perfect festival, expounding the culture, the sensitivity of a people who discover man's best anger, bile, and weeping. Neither in Spanish dance nor in the bullfight does anyone enjoy himself. The duende takes it upon himself to make us suffer by means of a drama of living forms, and clears the stairways for an evasion of the surrounding reality.

The duende works on the body of the dancer as the wind works on sand. With magical power he changes a girl into a lunar paralytic, or fills with adolescent blushes the broken old man begging in the wineshop, or make's a woman's hair smell like a nocturnal port, and he works continuously on the arms with expressions that are the mothers of the dances of every age.

But he can never repeat himself. This is interesting to emphasize: the duende does not repeat himself, any more than do the forms of the sea during a squall.

The duende is at his most impressive in the bullfight, for he must fight both death, which can destroy him, and geometry—measurement, the very basis of the festival.

The bull has his orbit and the bullfighter has his, and between these orbits is a point of danger, the vertex of the terrible play.

You can have muse with the muleta and angel with the banderillas and pass for a good bullfighter, but in the capework, when the bull is still clean of wounds, and at the moment of the kill, you need the duende's help to achieve artistic truth.

The bullfighter who scares the audience with his bravery is not bullfighting, but has ridiculously lowered himself to doing what anyone can do—gambling his life. But the torero who is bitten by duende gives a lesson in Pythagorean music and makes us forget he is always tossing his heart over the bull's horns.

From the crepuscule of the ring, Lagartijo with his Roman duende, Joselito with his Jewish duende, Belmonte with his baroque duende, and Cagancho with his Gypsy duende show poets, painters, musicians, and composers the four great roads of Spanish tradition.

Spain is the only country where death is a national spectacle, the only one where death sounds long trumpet blasts at the coming of spring,[16] and Spanish art is always ruled by a shrewd duende who makes it different and inventive.

The duende who for the first time in sculpture smears blood on the cheeks of the saints of Maestro Mateo de Compostela is the same one that makes Saint John of the Cross weep or burns naked nymphs in the sacred sonnets of Lope.

The duende that raises the tower of Sahagún or bakes hot bricks in

Calatayud or Teruel is the same one who breaks the clouds of El Greco and kicks Quevedo's constables and Goya's chimeras, sending them flying.

When he rains he brings duende-ridden Velázquez out from behind the monarchic grays where he is hiding. When he snows he makes Herrera take off his clothes to show that the cold does not kill.[17] When he burns he shoves Berruguete into his flames and makes him invent a new space for sculpture.

The muse of Góngora and the angel of Garcilaso must let go of their laurel garlands when the duende of Saint John of the Cross comes by, and

el ciervo vulnerado	the wounded stag
por el otero asoma.	comes to the hill.

The muse of Gonzalo de Berceo and the angel of the Arcipreste de Hita must withdraw to make way for Jorge Manrique mortally wounded at the doors of the castle of Belmonte. The muse of Gregorio Hernández and the angel of José de Mora must yield to the duende (crying tears of blood) of Pedro de Mena and to the duende (with the head of an Assyrian bull) of Martínez Montañéz; just as the melancholy muse of Catalonia and the dripping angel of Galicia look with love and wonder at the duende of Castile—the duende with its norms of clean-scrubbed sky and dry land, the angel and muse with their warm bread and gentle cow.

Duende of Quevedo and duende of Cervantes, one with green anemones of phosphorous and the other with blossoms of Ruidera gypsum, crown the reredos of the duende of Spain.[18]

Each art has a duende different in form and style, but their roots all meet in the place where the black sounds of Manuel Torre come from—the essence, the uncontrollable, quivering, common base of wood, sound, canvas, and word.

Behind those black sounds, tenderly and intimately, lives zephyrs, ants, volcanoes, and the huge night, straining its waist against the Milky Way.

Ladies and gentlemen, I have raised three arches and with clumsy hand have placed in them the angel, the muse, and the duende.

The muse stays still; she can have a minutely folded tunic or cow eyes like the ones that stare at us in Pompeii or the huge, four-faced nose her great friend Picasso has given her. The angel can shake the hair of Antonello da Messina, the tunic of Lippi, and the violin of Masolino or Rousseau.

The duende . . . Where is the duende? Through the empty arch comes a wind, a mental wind blowing relentlessly over the heads of the dead, in search of new landscapes and unknown accents; a wind that smells of baby's spittle, crushed grass, and jellyfish veil, announcing the constant baptism of newly created things.

HOLY WEEK IN GRANADA

The traveler who has no problems and is full of smiles and the screams of locomotives goes to the carnival of Valencia.[1] The bacchant goes to the Holy Week of Seville. The man burning for nudes goes to Málaga. But the melancholic and contemplative man goes to Granada, to be all alone in the breeze of sweet basil, dark moss, and trilling nightingales exhaled by the old hills near that bonfire of saffron, deep gray, and blotting-paper pink—the walls of the Alhambra. To be alone, to ponder an atmosphere full of difficult voices, in an air so beautiful it is almost thought, at a nerve center of Spain where the "meseta" poetry of Saint John of the Cross fills with cedars, cinnamons, and fountains, and Spanish mysticism can receive that Oriental air, that "wounded stag" (wounded by love) who "comes to the hill."

To be alone: to have the solitude one would want in Florence. To understand not the water's play, as at Versailles, but the water's passion, the water's agony.

Or to be with one's beloved and see how the spring pulses inside the trees and in the skin of the delicate marble columns, and how the yellow balls of the lemons climb through the glades and push back the frightened snow.

He who wants to feel the sweet ticktock of blood in his lips, next to the outer stamina of the bull, should be off to the baroque tumult of universal Seville. But whoever would like to sit down at a café table among phantasms and perhaps find a wonderful old ring somewhere along the corridors of his heart should go to the inner, hidden Granada. He will soon be surprised to learn there is no Holy Week in Granada. Holy Week does not suit the Christian, antispectacular spirit of her people. When I was a child I sometimes went to the Holy Burial. But only a few times, for the rich Granadans did not always want to spend their money on that parade.

These past few years, out of a desire to make money, they have put on processions wholly devoid of the seriousness and poetry of the Holy Week of my childhood. Back then it was a Holy Week of lace, of canaries flying amid the tapers, of an air that was sad and lukewarm, as if the whole day were asleep on the opulent throats of the old maids who promenaded on Holy Thursday pining for some soldier, judge, or foreign professor to carry them away someplace else. In those days the entire city was like a slow merry-go-round moving in and out of fantastically beautiful churches that were both fun houses and the apotheosis of the theater. Some of the altars were sown with wheat, others had little cascades, and some had the tenderness and poverty of a shooting gallery at a village fair. This one was nothing but reeds, like a celestial henhouse of firecrackers, and that one was immense, with the cruel purple, the sumptuous ermine of the poetry of Calderón.

In a house on the Calle de la Colcha, the street where wreaths and coffins are sold to poor people, the Roman soldaos would gather for practice. These "soldiers" were not a formal confraternity like the saucy armaos of the marvelous Macarena. They were hired hands—moving men, bootblacks, sick people just out of the hospital in need of a few dollars. They wore the red beards of Schopenhauer or of burning cats or ferocious professors. The captain was a military technician, and he taught them to mark the rhythm, which was like this—porón . . . chas!—and they would strike the ground with their lances in a deliciously funny way. As an example of Granada's natural genius, I will tell you that one year the Roman soldiers did not do very well at rehearsal and spent more than fifteen days furiously striking their lances on the ground before they could do it in unison. And then the captain shouted desperately, "Enough, enough! If you go on like this we'll be carrying the lances in candleholders!"—a saying very characteristic of Granada, and already commented upon by several generations.

I would like to ask my fellow Granadans to restore that old-fashioned

Holy Week and have the good taste to hide that hideous procession of the Last Supper, and not profane the Alhambra (which is not and never will be Christian) with the jangle of processions where false elegance mocks good taste and the crowd breaks laurels, tramples violets, and urinates by the hundred on the illustrious walls of poetry.

Granada must save for herself and for the traveler her inner Holy Week, the one that is so intimate and so silent that, I remember, a startled breeze from the Vega would enter the city by the Calle de la Gracia and would reach the fountain in the Plaza Nueva without hearing one noise or one song.

That way Granada's snowy spring will be perfect, and by means of the festival the intelligent traveler will be able to converse with her classic types: the human ocean of Ganivet, whose eyes are on the secret lilies of the Darro; the watcher of sunsets who climbs anxiously to the rooftop; the fellow who loves the Sierra as a form, without ever having gone near it; the dark beauty who yearns for love and sits by her mother in the garden; a whole admirable town of contemplatives who are surrounded by unique natural beauty, want nothing, and only know how to smile.

Amid an incredible variety of forms, landscape, light, and aromas, the uninformed traveler will get the feeling that Granada is the capital of a kingdom with its own art and literature, and he will find a curious mixture of Jewish Granada and Moorish Granada, which will seem to have been blended by Christianity but are really alive and incorruptible in their ignorance.

Neither the prodigious mound of the Cathedral nor the great imperial and Roman stamp of Carlos V have effaced the little shop of the Jew who prays before an image recast from the seven-branched candelabrum, just as the sepulchers of the Catholic Kings have not kept the Crescent from showing at times on the chest of Granada's finest sons. The dark struggle continues, without being expressed. Well, not without expression, because on the Colina Roja are two dead palaces, the Alhambra and the palace of Carlos V, which continue to fight the fatal duel throbbing in the heart of every Granadan.

All this the traveler should look at when he gets to Granada, which at this moment is putting on her long dress of springtime. As for the caravans of noisy tourists who like cabarets and luxury hotels—those frivolous groups that the people on the Albaicin call "Tio Turista"—to them the city's soul is closed.

SUN AND SHADE

Write these two nouns, like this, sun in black and shade in yellow, and you change the esthetics of the bullfight.[1] Perhaps that is how it must be, when you play with the sun and the shade, making them metaphor or concept.

This does not depend on any cloud, mirror, or wall, but on the bullfighter.

Sun and shade spring from the bullfighter.

Lagartijo achieved bullfights where there was only sun: the first glorious experimentation with a statuary esthetic, mortal and sensual like the bull before the banderillas. With Lagartijo the shade was pure simulation. He loved the nude and the concrete line, he loved the circumference of the sun and suppressed the infinite corner of the shade, terrible projected corner where wide rivers sound under the silent branches. Lagartijo explained and hardened the bulls' sun. For other bullfighters sun and shade continued to exist. Lagartijo's merit was to shuffle these two inimical elements in the solemn office of the corrida. Bombita learned to jump from one to the other without catching a cold. El Gallo knows how to close his eyes so they will not sicken during this quick passage. In contrast, how terribly the manly Machaquito used to bang into the dense wall of the shade! Bullfighters die in the ring because of these antagonistic halves. Before they tame the bull they must organize their postures in the inseparable day and night that embrace in the rondure. Between the yellow and the black is a dangerous play of distances; the air fills with concave and convex lens, and the bull swells and wanes, agile, dazzling, and uncertain, like a torch in the tower.

The bullfighter who does not know how to cross the line dividing the ring in two can fall down the stairs or lose his slippers for all time while passing from the brusque, stubborn sand that is hard as the gold coins of Carlos III to that other sand that is soft and difficult as the desert at night. It has always frightened me to see bullfighters in the shade drawing themselves erect for the kill. The shade is closed like a vertex and does not help them flee with precision. It gets in the way, as inert and heavy as a dead whale on the ocean.

But the sun is open on all four sides. Full of olés and burning serpents, its air makes the bullfighter conscious of his rhythm [illegible] and confident of his sword.

It was not till Belmonte arrived, dressed in green, ecstatic and full of the curved emotion of the tense bow, that the violent light of sun and shade could be theoretically suppressed. The embroidered jackets had become too brilliant, the sweating bull ran about the ring wearing fleeting vines of silver. The capes were leaving the same old images on the trembling dust. The bullring needed a rest, and it sighed for the light that comes through the ceilings of painters' studios.

So Belmonte, inspired draftsman, tamer of headless rhythms, succeeds in fighting by moonlight. When he comes into the ring the bullfight turns a perfect olive color, a dull color that snuffs out the systole and diastole of the fans. The bullring grows dim and splendidly drawn. Some of the spectators are wearing sandpaper suits, and when the man from Triana wheels around on his plinth, his chin nailed to his left nipple, their ovations are as furious and melancholy as a big rainstorm. Our heart feels the light of a cold moon. A cold moon shining on dying birds. Belmonte stands apart.

Without sun and without shade. Absorbing the bull as the swimmer absorbs the water and a child absorbs Sunday—sublime and tranquil, as moving as a crucifixion. If we look into the box seats at this moment we will see the majas hanging in suspense, their eyes wide open, their phosphorescent faces lit up as though by gas lamps.

THE POETIC IMAGE OF DON LUIS DE GÓNGORA

DEAR FRIENDS:

I am going to find it difficult to address you on such a complex, specialized subject as the poetry of Góngora.[1] But I want to do the best I can to entertain you for a while with the charming play of poetic emotion that is an inseparable part of the life of the cultivated man.

Naturally, I would not like this to be a bore. I have tried to give this talk various points of view, and of course to contribute something of my own to the criticism of the great Andalusian poet.

Before I begin, I suppose you know who Don Luis de Góngora was and can recognize a poetic image. You have all taken classes in literature and stylistics, and your professors, with rare and modern exceptions, have told you that Góngora was a very good poet who, for various reasons, suddenly became a very eccentric one (from an angel of light to an angel of darkness is the well-known phrase), and that he subjected the language to contortions and rhythms inconceivable to any sane mind. That is what they told you in high school, while eulogizing the insipid Núñez de Arce and Campoamor—poet of journalistic esthetics, of weddings, baptisms, burials, trips on the express train, etcetera—and the mediocre Zorrilla (not the magnificent Zorrilla of the plays and legends). My own literature teacher used to walk around the class and recite Zorrilla until his tongue hung out, to the intense amusement of us small fry.

Góngora has been furiously abused and ardently defended. His work palpitates today as though recently created. His glory is still causing arguments (a little shameful by now) and grumbling.

And a poetic image is always a transference of meaning.

Language is founded on images, and our people possess a magnificent wealth of them. To call the eaves of the roof an "alero" [literally, "wing of the roof"], to name a confection "bacon of heaven" or "nun's sighs" or a cupola a "half-orange"—and so on—these are all graceful, clever images. In Andalusia the images used in everyday speech are marvelously refined and sensitive, and their transformations are completely Gongoresque.

"Water ox" they call the deep channel of water that flows slowly across a field, thereby indicating its combativeness, its strength and volume. And I have heard a farmhand from Granada say, "Willow twigs always like to be on the tongue of the river." "Water ox" and "tongue of the river" are two popularly created images answering to a certain way of seeing things that is much like that of Don Luis de Góngora.

To situate Góngora we must enter into the history of Spanish lyrics and make note of two opposing groups: the poets called "popular" and (mistakenly) "national," on the one hand, and the poets correctly called "learned" or "courtly" on the other. People who make their poems as they walk the roads versus people who make their poems seated at the table, watching the roads through the leaded panes of the window. While in the thirteenth century, native, anonymous poets are stammering songs (now, alas, lost) of medieval Galician or Castillian sentiment, the group that we shall distinguish by calling "contrary" is attending to French and Provençal songs. Beneath a humid, golden sky are published the songbooks of Ajuda and the Vatican, where we can distinguish, through the Provençal rimes of King Diniz and through the cultured "cantigas de amigo" and "cantigas de amor" the tender voice of nameless poets engaged in pure song, free of grammar.

In the fifteenth century the Baena Songbook systematically rejects poetry of popular accent. But the Marquis of Santillana tells us that canciones de amigo were very fashionable among the young noblemen of his day.

And then the fresh breeze of Italy begins to blow.

The mothers of Garcilaso and Boscán cut orange blossoms for their weddings, but everywhere they are singing these already classical lines:

Al alba venid, buen amigo;	Come to the dawn, dear friend,
al alba venid.	come to the dawn.
Amigo el que yo más quería,	Friend that I wanted most,
venid a la luz del día.	come to the light of the day.
Amigo el que yo más amaba,	Friend that I loved the most,
venid a la luz del alba.	come to the light of dawn.
Venid a la luz del día,	Come to the light of day,
non trayáis compañía.	do not bring company.
Venid a la luz del alba,	Come to the light of dawn,
non trayáis gran compaña.	do not bring much company.

And just as Garcilaso is bringing us the hendecasyllabic line with its perfumed gloves, music comes to the aid of the popularists. The *Cancionero musical de Palacio* is published, and the popular style comes into vogue. The musicians cull amatory, pastoral, and chivalresque songs from oral tradition. On pages made for aristocratic eyes we hear the voices of ruffians in taverns and shepherd girls from Avila, the ballad of the Moor with the long beard, sweet cantos de amigo, the monotonous oracles of the blind man, the song of the knight lost in the thicket, and the exquisite lament of the peasant girl who has been seduced and abandoned—a refined, exact landscape of what is picturesque and spiritual and Spanish.

The illustrious Menéndez Pidal says that "humanism opened the eyes of the learned to a deep understanding of the human spirit in all its manifestations, and brought popular art the intelligent attention it deserved but had never gotten." Proof of this was the cultivation of the "vihuela" and of popular songs by great musicians like the Valencian Luis Milán, who translated Castiglione's *Courtier,* and Francisco Salinas, the friend of Fray Luis de León.

The two groups declared open war on each other. Cristóbal de Castillejo and Gregorio Silvestre, with their love of the popular tradition, took up the Castilian banner. Followed by a larger group, Garcilaso affirmed his allegiance to what was called "Italian taste." And when, in the last months of 1609, Góngora writes the "Panegyric to the Duke of Lerma," the war between the partisans of the refined Cordovan and the friends of the tireless Lope de Vega reaches a level of exaltation and daring that is unparalleled in any literary epoch. Partisans of the dark style ("tenebrosistas") and those of the plain style ("llanistas") wage a lively, amusing, sometimes dramatic, and almost always obscene war of sonnets.

But I would like to make clear that I do not believe in the efficacy of this fight, nor in this business about Italianist versus Castilian poets. In all of them, I think, there is profound national feeling. The undeniable foreign influence does not weigh heavily on their spirits. To classify them is simply a question of historic focus. Garcilaso is as national as Castillejo. Castillejo is imbued with the Middle Ages, he is an archaistic poet whose taste has just become outmoded. On the banks of the Tagus, Garcilaso, a man of the Renaissance, unearths ancient mythologies clouded by Time, with a genuine Spanish gallantry, discovered only then, and an eternally Spanish word.

Lope gathers the lyrical archaisms of the late Middle Ages and creates a profoundly romantic theater, the child of its time. The great and relatively recent maritime discoveries (pure romanticism) stare him in the face. His theater of love, adventure, and the duel prove him a man of national tradition. But Góngora is just as "national" as Lope. In his characteristic, definitive work Góngora flees the chivalresque and medieval tradition, searching profoundly (not superficially like Garcilaso) for the glorious, ancient Latin tradition. He searches the lonely air of Córdoba for the voices of Seneca and Lucan. And modeling Castilian verses by the cold light of the Roman lamp, he carries to its apogee a type of art uniquely Spanish: baroque. It has been an intense battle between medievalists and Latinists: poets who love the picturesque and local versus poets of the court; poets who muffle their faces versus poets who look for the nude. But the ordered, sensual breeze sent by the Italian Renaissance does not reach any of their hearts. They are either romantics, like Lope and Herrera, or Catholic and baroque, like Góngora and Calderón. Geography and Heaven conquer the Library.

This is where I wanted my brief summary to take me. I have tried to trace Góngora's lineage, in order to place him in his aristocratic solitude.

"Much has been written about Góngora, but the genesis of his poetic reform remains obscure . . ." That is how the most modern and most prudent grammarians start out when they speak of the father of modern lyric poetry. I will not mention Menéndez Pelayo, who never understood Góngora, because he did understand everybody else so prodigiously well.

Other critics, with certain historical justification, attribute what they call Góngora's sudden change to the theories of Ambrosio de Morales; the suggestions of his teacher Herrera; the reading of a book by Luis Carrillo (apologist of the obscure style), and to other causes that seem reasonable. But the Frenchman M. Lucien-Paul Thomas attributes it to a brain disorder, and Mr. Fitzmaurice-Kelly, demonstrating the critical incapacity that distinguishes him whenever he writes about an unclassified author, is inclined to believe that the poet wrote the *Solitudes* merely to call attention to his literary personality. Nothing funnier than these serious opinions. And nothing more irreverent.

In Spain Góngora the "cultist" has been—and still is—considered a monster of grammatical vices whose poetry lacks all the fundamental elements of beauty. The most eminent grammarians and teachers of style have considered the *Solitudes* an embarrassing scar. Dark, stupid voices have been raised, lacking light and spirit, to anathematize what they proclaim obscure and empty. They were able to corner Góngora and to throw dirt into new eyes just beginning to understand him, and for two long centuries they have told us, "Keep away from him. He is incomprehensible." Góngora has stood alone like a leper covered with sores of cold silver light, a fresh-cut branch in his hands, awaiting the new generations who will claim his legacy of objectivity and his sense of metaphor.

It is a problem of understanding. You must not read Góngora, you must study him. He does not come looking for us, as do other poets, to make us melancholy; we have to pursue him rationally. Góngora cannot be understood on the first reading. A work of philosophy may be understood by no more than a few people without anyone calling its author obscure. But that is far from being the case in poetry. Or so it seems.

What were the causes of Góngora's revolution? Causes? An inborn necessity for fresh beauty made him cast language in a new way. He was from Córdoba, and he knew Latin like almost no one else. Do not look for it in history, look for it in his soul. Góngora invented a new method, unprecedented in Spanish, for hunting and molding metaphors, and thought, without saying so, that the eternity of a poem depends on the quality and perfect fit of its images.

Since then, Marcel Proust has written that only metaphor can give style a sort of eternity.

His need for new beauty and his boredom with the poetic production of his day made Góngora develop a keen, almost unbearable critical sensibility. He nearly came to despise poetry.

He could no longer create poems for the old Castilian taste; he no longer enjoyed the heroic simplicity of the ballad. When, so as not to work, he took a look at the literary spectacle around him, he found it full of defects, imperfections, and vulgar sentiments. All the dust of Castile was covering his soul and his prebendary's cassock. He felt that the poems of others were imperfect and careless, as though written off the cuff.

And tired of Castilians and of "local color," he read his Virgil, delighting in it, a man thirsty for elegance. His sensitivity made his eyes into a microscope. He saw the Castilian language lame and full of gaps, and with his fragrant aesthetic instinct he began to construct a new tower of gems and invented stones that chafed the pride of the Castilians in their palaces of adobe. He recognized the fleetingness of human feeling and the weakness of the spontaneous expressions which can move us only at certain moments, and he wanted the beauty of his work to emanate from the metaphor purified of realities that die, metaphor built with a sculptor's spirit and placed in the stratosphere.

He loved objective beauty—pure, useless beauty, devoid of communicable anxieties.

While everyone else asks for bread, Góngora asks for the precious stone of each day. Without any sense of real reality, but the absolute master of poetic reality. What did the poet do to give his aesthetic credo unity and true proportions? He limited himself. He examined his conscience and, with all his critical capacity, studied the mechanics of his creation.

A poet must be a professor of the five bodily senses, in this order: sight, touch, hearing, smell, and taste. And in order to master the most beautiful images, he must open doors between all of them. He must frequently superimpose one sensation on another and even mask its features.

And thus Góngora can say in his "First Solitude":[2]

Pintadas aves—cítaras de pluma—
coronaban la bárbara capilla,
mientras el arroyuelo para oílla
hace de blanca espuma
tantas orejas cuantas guijas lava.

Above, the feathered lyres,
The painted linnets, crowned
The untaught rustic choirs;
Meanwhile the stream a means to hear them found,
Shaping in ears the milk-white foam around
The pebbles in its course,
From where it rose to where it lost its force.

And he can say, describing a shepherdess:

Del verde margen otra las mejores rosas traslada y lirios al cabello, o por lo matizado, o por lo bello si aurora no con rayos, sol con flores.	From the green margin, one Roses transferred and lilies to her hair, And, by the bloom of color or the fair, Seemed, if no tinted dawn, a flowering sun.

Or:

de las ondas el pez con vuelo mudo   from the waves, the fish, in silent flight

Or:

verdes voces   green voices

Or:

voz pintada, canto alado,   painted voice, winged song,

Or:

órgano de pluma.   organ of feathers.

In order to live, a metaphor needs two elements, form and a radius of action. A central nucleus and the perspective surrounding it. The nucleus opens like the flower that startles us by its strangeness; but within the radius of light we learn the name of the flower, and we get to know its perfume. The metaphor is always ruled by sight (at times by sublimated sight); it is sight that limits it and supplies its reality. Even the most evanescent [*sic*] English poets, like Keats, need to sketch and limit their metaphors and figures, and Keats's admirable plasticity *saves him* from the dangerous poetic world of visions. "Poesy alone can tell her dreams," he exclaims. Sight prevents shadow from muddying the contours of the image.

No one who has been blind from birth can be a plastic poet of objective images, because he has no idea of Nature's proportions. The blind man is better off in the endless, luminous field of mysticism, devoid of real objects and combed by long breezes of wisdom.

So then, all images blossom in the field of sight.

Touch reveals the quality of the lyric materials, quality that is almost . . . *pictorial.* And the images which the other senses construct are subject to sight and touch.

The metaphor is an exchange of clothes, ends, or occupations among natural objects or ideas. It has its planes and orbits. The metaphor unites two antagonistic worlds by means of an equestrian leap of the imagination. The cinematographer Jean Epstein says that it is a "theorem in which one jumps directly from the hypothesis to the conclusion." Exactly.

The originality of Don Luis de Góngora, apart from grammar, is in his method of *hunting* images, which he invented. He studied these images using his dramatic powers of self-criticism. A man with an amazing capacity for myth, he studies the beautiful conceptions of the ancients and, fleeing the mountains and their luminous visions, he sits down on the shores of the sea where the wind

le corre, en lecho azul de aguas marinas,	draws round him on the blue couch of the sea,
turquesadas cortinas.	turquoise curtains.

And there he ties down and bridles his imagination, as though he were a sculptor, in order to begin his poem. So greatly does he want to dominate it and round it off that he unconsciously loves islands, for he thinks, with good reason, that a man can possess and govern, better than any other piece of land, the defined, visible orb that is limited by water. His imaginative machinery is perfect. There are times when each image is a created myth.

Góngora molds and harmonizes the most dissimilar worlds in a way that sometimes borders on violence. In his hands there is neither disorder or disproportion. He picks up oceans, geographical realms, and hurricane winds and plays with them like toys. He unites astronomical sensations with tiny details of infinitesimal things, with a sense for masses and materials that had been unknown to poetry. In his "First Solitude" (lines 34–41) he says:

Naked the youth, that ocean which before
His raiment drank, he gave back to the shore;

And then the garments to the sun he spread,
Which, with its gentle tongue of temperate fire,
Slowly attacked, but with no fierce desire,
The least wave sipping from the smallest thread.

Desnudo el joven, cuanto ya el vestido
Océano ha bebido,
restituir le hace a las arenas;
y al Sol le extiende luego,
que, lamiéndolo apenas
su dulce lengua de templado fuego
lento lo embiste y con süave estilo
la menor onda chupa al menor hilo.

What a sure touch Góngora shows in harmonizing the Ocean, the Sun (that golden dragon fencing with its tepid tongue), and the lad's wet clothes, as the blind head of the star sips "the least wave . . . from the smallest thread"! There are more nuances in these six lines than in fifty octaves of Tasso's *Gerusalemme Liberata,* and each detail is studied and felt as in the work of a jeweler. Nothing could better convey the sensation of a sinking, weightless Sun than these lines:

que, lamiéndolo apenas	that, hardly licking him,
....	....
lento lo embiste	slowly attacks him

Because Góngora has tied up his imagination, he can detain it at will, and does not allow himself to be dragged about by the dark natural forces of the law of inertia, nor by the fleeting mirages where careless poets die like moths in a lamp. There are moments in the *Solitudes* that are incredible. It is a mystery how Góngora can play with these great masses and geographical terms without falling into something truly monstrous or into disagreeable hyperbole.

In the inexhaustible "First Solitude" he says, referring to the Isthmus of Suez [Panama]:

The isthmus with a hundred feathers armed;
This land their proper limit has assigned
Unto the (crystal serpent) ocean tides,

And from the head, crowned by the North, divides
The tail the South with stars antarctic scaled.

el istmo que al Océano divide,
y—sierpe de cristal—juntar le impide
la cabeza, del Norte coronada,
con la que ilustra el Sur cola escamada
de antárticas estrellas.

Remember the left-hand wing of the map of the world.

Or he sketches these two winds, with the surest hand, in exact proportion:

For Auster on wings that never parch
For Boreas puffing through a hundred mouths

para el Austro de alas nunca enjutas,
para el Cierzo espirante por cien bocas.

Or he composes this fitting poetic definition of the Straits of Magellan:

the elusive hinge of silver fine . . .
Hinge that unites, one ocean, the two seas,
Whether the carpet of the morning star
It kisses, or the rocks of Hercules.

cuando halló de fugitiva plata
la bisagra, aunque estrecha, abrazadora
de un Océano y otro siempre uno.

Or he calls the fisherman:

Bárbaro observador, mas diligente	Savage but diligent observer
de las inciertas formas de la Luna.	of the uncertain forms of the Moon.

Or, in the "First Solitude," he compares the islands of Oceania with the nymphs of Diana the Huntress in the backwaters of the Eurotas:

That fixed armada in the eastern sea
Of islands firm I cannot well describe,

Whose number, though for no lasciviousness
But for their sweetness and variety,
The beautiful confusion emulate
When in the white pools of Eurotas rose
The virginal and naked hunting tribe . . .

De firmes islas no la inmóvil flota
de aquel mar del Alba te describo,
cuyo número—ya que no lascivo—
por lo bello agradable y por lo vario
la dulce confusión hacer podía
que en los blancos estanques del Eurota
la virginal desnuda montería . . .

But what is interesting is that Góngora treats small objects and forms with the same love, the same poetic greatness as he does large ones. An apple is just as intense to him as the ocean, a bee just as surprising as a forest. He places himself in front of nature and admires, with penetrating eyes, the identical beauty of all forms. He enters what might be called the world of each thing, and, once there, proportions his feeling to the feelings which surround him. An apple means no more to him than an ocean because he knows that each is infinite in its own world. The life of an apple, from when it is a tenuous blossom until it falls golden from the tree to the grass, is just as mysterious, just as great as the periodic rhythm of the tides. And a poet ought to know this. The greatness of a poem does not depend on the magnitude of its theme, nor on its proportion or sentiments. One could easily make an epic poem about the passionate struggle of the leucocytes in the imprisoned branches of the veins, and the form and fragrance of just one rose can be made to render an impression of infinity.

Góngora treats all his materials alike. He wields seas and continents like a Cyclops, but goes on to analyze fruits and objects. In fact, small things entertain him and excite him even more than large ones.

In the tenth stanza of the *Fable of Polyphemus and Galatea* he says:

Golden cradle of the pear, the tawny straw,
pale governess, denies her ward, from greed,
and generously gilds her.

la pera, de quien fue cuna dorada
la rubia paja y—pálida tutora—
la niega avara y pródiga la dora.

He calls the straw "pale governess" of the fruit because in her bosom the fruit (taken from its mother, the branch, while still green) finishes ripening. "Pale governess" who "denies her ward, from greed, and generously gilds her," since the straw hides the pear from the gaze of others in order to dress her in gold.

On another occasion he writes:

Few paces distant, no less wondered he
At a small hill with laurels on its brow,
   Which from its bosom now
Dismissed its population festively,
Its coneys that the wind allowed that day
To scurry forth to tread on flowers and play.

montecillo, las sienes laureado,
traviesos despidiendo moradores
   de sus confusos senos,
conejuelos que, el viento consultado,
salieron retozando a pisar flores.

The way the animals pull up short, the grimace they make on leaving their burrows are described with real grace:

[Literally:] Its coneys that, having consulted the wind,
Scurry forth to tread on flowers.

conejuelos que, el viento consultado,
salieron retozando a pisar flores.

But even more significant are these lines about a beehive in the trunk of a tree, the fortress, Góngora says, of

A rustling Amazon, winged Dido she,
Though of a more chaste army, and more fair
Republic, girded, by no ramparts' screen,

But cork-bark; in this Carthage, then, behold
The bee as queen who shines with wandering gold;
Either the sap she drinks from the pure air,
Or else the exudation of the skies
That sip the spittle from each silent star.

que sin corona vuela y sin espada,
susurrante amazona, Dido alada,
de ejército más casto, de más bella
República, ceñida, en vez de muros,
de cortezas; en esta, pues, Cartago,
reina la abeja, oro brillando vago,
o el jugo bebe de los aires puros,
o el sudor de los cielos, cuando liba
de las mudas estrellas la saliva.

Those lines have an almost epic greatness. And the poet is writing about a bee and its hive! "Republic, girded by no ramparts' screen, / But cork bark," he says of the sylvan hive. He affirms that the bee, "rustling Amazon," drinks the juice of the pure air, and he calls the dew "spittle of the flowers" and the flowers "silent stars." Isn't Góngora just as great here as when he tells us of the sea or the dawn, using astronomical terms? He is always doubling and tripling the image to carry us off to different levels where he can perfect the sensation and connect it with all its other aspects. No "pure poetry" could be more surprising!

Góngora had classical learning which gave him faith in himself and allowed him to say, in the seventeenth century:

Las horas ya de números vestidas	The hours now dressed in numbers

(incredible image of the clock), or call a grotto, without naming it, a "melancholy yawn of the earth." Of all his contemporaries, only Quevedo can come up with such expressions, from time to time. But Quevedo's are not of the same quality. It was not until the nineteenth century that Góngora found his best disciple, one who did not even know him, the great poet and hallucinated professor Stéphane Mallarmé, who promenaded his unexcelled abstract lyricism down the rue de Rome and opened up the ventilated and violent road of the new poetic schools. The two of them love the same swans, mirrors, hard lights, and feminine tresses, both have the fixed tremor of the baroque, but Góngora is stronger, with a verbal wealth unknown to Mallarmé and a sense of ecstatic beauty that cannot be seen in the works of the moderns with their humorism and poisoned needle of irony.

Naturally, Góngora does not create his images directly from nature. He carries the object, thing, or act to the camera obscura of his cerebrum. From there, transformed, it leaps back into and coalesces with the other world. Because his poetry is indirect, one cannot read it in front of the objects he is talking about. The spiritual Cordovan's roses, black poplars, shepherd lads, and seas are newly created. The sea is a "rough emerald set in marble, always undulous," and the black poplar is a "green lyre." But what could be more stupid than to read the madrigal to a rose with a live rose in your hand! One or the other is unnecessary.

Like any great poet, Góngora possesses a world apart, a world of the essential features and quiddities of things.

The poet who is about to make a poem (and I know this from experience) has the vague feeling he is going on a nocturnal hunting trip in an incredibly distant forest. An inexplicable fear murmurs in his heart. In order to calm down, it is always a good idea to take a glass of fresh water and to make meaningless black marks with your pen. I say black because, and this is a secret . . . I do not use colored ink. The poet goes on a hunt. Delicate breezes cool the crystals of his eyes. The moon, round as a horn of soft metal, sounds in the silence of the highest branches. White stags appear between the tree trunks. The whole night takes shelter beneath a screen of murmurs. Deep, serene waters sparkle among the rushes. One must set out. And this is the dangerous moment for the poet. The poet ought to carry a map of the places he is going to visit, and he ought to be serene as he faces the thousand beauties and thousand uglinesses posing as beauties that must pass before his eyes. He ought to cover his ears like Ulysses; to shoot his arrows at the living metaphor and not the make-believe or false ones that are nearby. It is a dangerous moment, for if the poet surrenders he will never be able to raise up his work. The poet must go to the hunt immaculate and serene, disguised even. He must firmly resist mirages and must carefully ambush the real, palpitant flesh that harmonizes with the map of the poem he has already glimpsed. At times one must cry out in the poetic solitude to drive away the facile evil spirits that would hand us over to popular adulation devoid of esthetic meaning, order, or beauty. Góngora is better prepared than anyone for this interior hunt. Neither pale nor colored images nor overly brilliant ones can frighten him in his mental landscape. He hunts the image that no one else sees (so unrelated does it seem to anything else), the white, straggling image that livens his startling poetical moments. His fantasy counts on his five bodily senses; they obey him blindly, like five colorless slaves, and do not cheat him as they do other mortals. He clearly intuits that the nature that God made is not the nature that ought to live in poems, and he orders his landscapes by analyzing their components. We might say that he puts nature and all her hues and colors through the discipline of the musical scale. He says in the *"Second Solitude"* (lines 350–60):

> The water, on the many boulders breaking,
> Tones of a crystal theorbo was making,
> And the confusedly agreeing choirs,
> Among the spirals of the ivy green,
> Were many, many times winged Muses nine,
>   (Their feathers light the screen
> Deceitful that concealed their curvèd lyres)
> That sweet although uncertain meters told
>   In language manifold;
> While, supping mid the porphyry, combined
>   Three Sirens' flattery,
> Offered unto the Jupiter of sea.

>   Rompida el agua en las menudas piedras,
> cristalina sonante era tïorba,
> y las confusamente acordes aves
> entre las verdes roscas de las yedras
> muchas eran, y muchas veces nueve
> aladas musas, que—de pluma leve
> engañada su oculta lira corva—
> metros inciertos, sí, pero süaves,
> en idïomas cantan diferentes;
> mientras, cenando en pórfidos lucientes,
>   lisonjean apenas
> al Júpiter marino tres sirenas.

What an admirable way to organize the choir of birds:

Were many, many times winged Muses nine

Muchas eran, y muchas veces nueve
aladas musas . . .

And what a charming way to say that they were of many different species:

Metros inciertos, sí, pero süaves, en idiomas cantan diferentes.	sweet although uncertain meters told In language manifold

Elsewhere he says:

Terno de gracias bello, repetido cuatro veces en doce labradoras, entró bailando numerosamente.	Triads of graces these Four times repeated in twelve maidens . . . Who entered dancing to that melody

The great French poet Paul Valéry says that the state of inspiration is not the right one in which to write a poem. Because I believe in the inspiration sent by God, I think Valéry is on the right track. Inspiration is a state of collection, not creative dynamism. One must allow one's vision of the concept to settle and clear. I do not think any great artist works in a fever. Even the mystics get to work only after the ineffable dove of the Holy Spirit has already left their cells and is losing itself in the clouds. One returns from inspiration as from a foreign country. The poem is the narration of the voyage. Inspiration supplies the image, but not its dress, and to give it that dress one must observe—calmly and dispassionately—the quality and sonority of words. One does not know which to admire more in Góngora, his poetic substance or its inimitable, highly inspired form. His letter gives life to his spirit, instead of killing it. He is not spontaneous, but he is fresh and young. He is not easy, but he is luminous and intelligent. Even when he uses hyperbole too excessively, and this is rare, he does so with such typical Andalusian charm that we laugh and admire him all the more: his hyperbole is the flattery of the Cordovan who is always falling in love.

He says of a bride:

. . . such a beautiful young virgin, she
—Herself the Aurora of her sovereign eyes—

Could warm with her two suns Norwegian lands,
and whiten Ethiopia with two hands.

Virgen tan bella que hacer podría
tórrida la Noruega con dos soles
y blanca la Etiopia con dos manos.

Pure Andalusian flattery; The marvelous gallantry of a man who has crossed the Guadalquivir on a full-blooded colt. In this Góngora shows the full range of his fantasy.

And now let us look at this "obscurity" of Góngora. What is all this about obscurity? I think his sin was lucidity. But to reach him one must be initiated into poetry; one's sensibility must be prepared by reading and experience. Whoever is outside his world cannot savor it, just as he does not savor a picture though he knows what it represents, or a musical composition. You must not read Góngora, you must love him. The critical grammarians, burdened by the constructions they alone know, have not admitted the fecund revolution brought by Góngora, just as the Beethovenians, petrified in their rotten ecstasies say that the music of Claude Debussy is a cat walking on the piano. They have not admitted the grammatical revolution, but the Spanish language, which has nothing to do with them, received it with open arms. With Góngora new words blossomed. Castilian acquired new perspectives. A life-giving dew fell; that is what a great poet always is to a language. In this grammatical context the case of Góngora is unique. The old intellectuals who liked to read the poetry of their age were probably stupefied to see Castilian turning into a foreign language they could not decipher.

Quevedo, irritated and at bottom envious, engaged Góngora in battle with this sonnet called "Recipe for Making 'Solitudes,' " in which he ridicules the strange curse words and gibberish of Don Luis. It goes like this:

He who'd become a Cultist in one day
need only learn some nonsense words like these:
palestra, pulse, erect, and harmonies,
a little much, incisures, cede, convey.

If not aduncal, yes and if indeed,
canorous, liberate, ostent, libate,

interstice, purpuraceous, conculcate,
neutrality, nocturnal, pyre, impede.

Signals, juvent, fruster, pore, and argent,
candor, prescient, construct, meter, altern,
meta, harpy, mental, emulate.

Use much liquid, add a little errant,
not to mention livor, fulgor, cavern.
Don't forget a dash of arrogate.

Quien quisiere ser culto en sólo un día,
la jeri—aprenderá—gonza siguiente:
Fulgores, arrogar, joven, presiente,
candor, construve, métrica armonía.

Poco, mucho, si no, purpuracía,
neutralidad, conculca, erige, mente,
pulsa, ostenta, librar, adolescente,
señas traslada, pira, frustra, harpía.

Cede, impide, cisuras, petulante,
palestra, liba, meta, argento, alterna,
si bien disuelve émulo canoro.

Use mucho de líquido y de errante,
su poco de nocturno y de caverna.
Anden listos livor, adunco, y poro.

What a wonderful party of color and music for the Castilian language. This is the gibberish of Don Luis de Góngora y Argote. Had Quevedo known he was really eulogizing his enemy, he would have packed his dense, burning melancholy off to the Castilian wastelands of the Torre de Juan Abad. More than Cervantes, Góngora can be called the father of the Castilian tongue, and yet until this year the Spanish Academy had not declared him an "Authority of the Language."

One thing that made Góngora obscure to his contemporaries, his language, no longer presents a problem. There are no longer any unknown words in his exquisite vocabulary. That leaves his syntax and his mythological transformations.

His sentences, when one rearranges them like Latin paragraphs, become clear. His mythological world *is* difficult to understand, partly because almost nobody knows any mythology and partly because Góngora is never content just to cite a myth, he must transform it or allude to it obliquely. This is where his metaphors acquire an inimitable tone. Hesiod tells his *Theogony* with popular and religious fervor. The subtle Cordovan retells it, stylizing it or inventing altogether new myths. This is where he really swipes his poetic paw, this is where you find his most daring transformations and his disdain for the explicative method.

Jupiter, in the form of a bull with golden horns, rapes the nymph Europe:

> It was the flowery season of the year
> In which Europa's perjured robber strays
> —Whose brow the arms of the half-moon adorn
>
> Era del año la estación florida
> en que el mentido robador de Europa,
> media luna las armas de su frente . . .

"Perjured robber"! What a delicate way to describe the disguised god! He also mentions

> the canorous sound
> Of her before a nymph but now a reed
>
> el canoro
> son de la ninfa un tiempo, ahora caña,

referring to the nymph Syrinx, whom the god Pan, after being rejected by her, angrily turned into a reed that later became a seven-tone flute.

Or he transforms the myth of Icarus in this curious manner:

> Once my audacious thought,
> In feathers clad, to scale the zenith sought;
> Though its bold flight assigned
> No second name unto a spumy wave,
> The dress of feathers gave
> The record of the dizzy fall to mind
> To the pellucid annals of the wind.

Audaz mi pensamiento
el cenit escaló, plumas vestido,
  cuyo vuelo atrevido
—si no ha dado su nombre a tus espumas—
de sus vestidas plumas
conservarán el desvanecimiento
los anales diafanos del viento.

Or he describes Juno's peacocks and their gaudy feathers like this:

pious volants,
whose feathers are blue eyes
with lashes of gold, conduct the high goddess,
chief glory of the sovereign choir.

volantes pías
que azules ojos con pestañas de oro
sus plumas son, conduzcan alta diosa
gloria mayor del soberano coro.

Or, rightly taking away its epithet of "pure," he calls the dove

Ave lasciva de la cipria Diosa. Lascivious fledgling of the Cypriote queen.

Góngora proceeds by allusions. He places myths in profile, showing only one aspect of them and concealing them among other, distinct images. In mythology, Bacchus suffers three passions and deaths. He is first a goat with twisting horns. For love of his dancer Cyssus, who dies and is turned into ivy, Bacchus changes into a vine. Lastly, he dies and is turned into a fig tree. And so Bacchus is thrice born. Góngora alludes to these transformations in a "Solitude" in a way that is delicate and profound, but comprehensible only to those who are in on the story.

Six poplars black, by ivies six embraced,
Were thrysi of the Greek god, who was born
A second time, who with vine-shoots conceals
Upon his brow each horn . . .

Seis chopos de seis yedras abrazados
tirsos eran del griego dios, nacido

segunda vez, que en pámpanos desmiente
  los cuernos de su frente.

The Bacchus of the bacchanal, near his love, who is stylized in embracing ivy, *conceals* under his crown of grape leaves his scandalous old horns.

And this is the form of all the "cultist" poems. Góngora has developed such keen theogonic feeling that he turns everything he touches into myth. The elements of his landscapes act as though they were gods of unlimited power unknown to men. He gives them hearing and feeling. He creates them. In the "Second Solitude" there is a foreigner, a young man, who while rowing his little boat and singing the most tender amorous lament makes

His instrument the boat, a string each oar

instrumento el bajel, cuerdas los remos.

The lover thinks that he is alone in the middle of the water's green solitude, but the sea hears him, the winds hear him, and finally the echo saves the "sweetest" but "the least clear" syllable of his song:

The ocean is not deaf. Our learning feigns.
Although sometimes, enraged, it either hears
No pilot's voice, or savagely replies;
But now serene it simulated ears
More than the stranger sowed sad harmonies
—Canorous peasant he—on wavy plains.
  Spongy the sea and dumb,
  It drank the tearful lay,
Whose numbers sweet in no small tuneful sum
  The wind then stole away
In the gyrations of the feathers there
That wings invisible feigned in the air;
Echo, who in a concave rock was decked,
Sought, curious, and, like a miser, kept
The sweetest, though perhaps not the least clear
  Syllable, till ere long
Sight of the hovels made an end to song.

No es sordo el mar; la erudición engaña.
    Bien que tal vez sañudo
no oya al piloto, o le responda fiero,
sereno disimula más orejas
    que sembró dulces quejas
—canoro labrador—el forastero,
    en su undosa campaña.
Espongïoso, pues, se bebió y mudo
el lagrimoso reconocimiento,
de cuyos dulces números no poca
    concentuosa suma
en los dos giros de invisible pluma
que fingen sus dos alas hurtó el viento;
Eco—vestida una cavada roca—
solicitó curiosa y guardó avara
la más dulce—si no la menos clara—
    sílaba, siendo en tanto
la vista de las chozas fin del canto.

This way of animating and vivifying Nature is characteristic of Góngora. He needs the elements to be conscious. He hates what is deaf, he hates dark forces that have no limits. He is a monolithic poet whose esthetics are unalterable and dogmatic.

Another time the sea sings in the mouth of a river, and

    now a spumy centaur, see
—Half sea, half estuary—
Twice in a day tread underfoot the plain,
Pretending too to scale the mount, in vain . . .

Centauro ya espumoso el Oceano
    —medio mar, medio ría—
dos veces huella la campaña al día,
pretendiendo escalar el monte en vano.

His inventiveness is unperturbed and utterly without chiaroscuro. So that when in the *Polyphemus* he invents a myth about pearls, he says of the foot of Galatea touching the shells:

her foot whose beautiful contact makes them
without conceiving dew give birth to pearls.

cuyo bello contacto puede hacerlas,
sin concebir rocío, parir perlas.

We have already seen how the poet transforms all that he touches. His sublime theogonic feeling gives personality to the forces of nature. And his erotic feeling toward women (which he had to hide because of his clerical habit) and his gallantry are stylized until they reach inviolable heights. The *Fable of Polyphemus and Galatea* is a poem of extreme eroticism. One could say that it has a floral sexuality, sexuality of stamen and pistil in the emotional flight of pollen in the spring.

And when has a kiss ever been described so naturally, harmoniously, and innocently as here in the *Polyphemus:*

Cupid has not allowed the doves
to join the rubies of their two beaks
when the bold young man
sucks the two carmine leaves.
As many black violets as Paphus produces
Are Gnidus' white ones.
They rain on him whom Love wants
to be the thalamus of Acis and Galatea.

No a las palomas concedió Cupido
juntar de sus dos picos los rubíes,
cuando al clavel el joven atrevido
las dos hojas le chupa carmesíes.
Cuantas produce Pafo, engendra Gnido
negras violas, blancos alhelíes,
llueven sobre el que Amor quiere que sea
tálamo de Acis y de Galatea.

It is sumptuous, it is exquisite, but not, in itself obscure. It is we who are obscure, we have no capacity to penetrate Góngora's intelligence. The mystery is not outside of us, we carry it on our hearts. We ought not to speak of an obscure thing, but of an obscure man. Góngora never wanted to be turbid, he wanted to be clear, iridescent, elegant. He does not like penumbra or deformed metaphors. On the contrary, in his own way he explains things to perfection. He ends by making his poem a great still life.

During his poetic life Góngora was faced with a problem and managed to solve it. Until then, it had been held impossible to make a grand lyric poem, as opposed to the dozens of long epics. How could one maintain pure lyric tension over whole squadrons of verses? How do so without narration? One slip and the poem would turn into an epic, that is if the narration, the anecdote were allowed any importance. And if it did not narrate anything, wouldn't the poem break into a thousand senseless parts? Góngora chooses his story and covers it with metaphors. The story becomes hard to find. It is transformed. It is the poem's skeleton, clothed in the magnificent flesh of the images. Each moment has its own identical intensity and plastic value. The anecdote has no importance except that its invisible thread gives the poem unity. Góngora writes a great lyric poem of unheard-of proportions—the *Solitudes.*

And this great poem sums up all the lyrical-pastoral sentiment of the Spanish poets who came before him. The bucolic dream that Cervantes dreamed and could never quite get down; the Arcadia that Lope de Vega could not show in lasting light—these were the dreams that Góngora drew so boldly. The countryside, half garden, amiable countryside of soft breezes and garlands and cultured but shy shepherdesses, the place glimpsed by every poet of the sixteenth and seventeenth centuries, is realized in Góngora's first and second "Solitudes." This is the aristocratic, mythological landscape Don Quixote was dreaming of at the hour of his death. An orderly countryside where poetry measures and governs its delirium.

The professors of literature say that there are two Góngoras—the "cultist" and the plain one. But anyone with a little perception and even a jot of sensibility will notice, as he analyzes Góngora's work, that Góngora's image is always "cultist." Even in the simplest "romancillos" his metaphors and figures of speech come from the same mechanism he employs in his genuinely "cultist" work. But there they are situated in clear anecdote or simple landscape, while in the "cultist" works they are tied to other images that are tied to still others. Whence the apparent difficulty.

Here the examples are infinite. In one of his first poems, from the year 1580, he says:

Los rayos le cuenta al sol	Beautiful Jacinta one day
con un peine de marfil	counts the rays of the sun
la bella Jacinta, un día.	with a comb of ivory.

Or he says:

La mano oscurece al peine.	The hand darkens the comb.

Or, in a romancillo, speaking of a young man:

Las veinas con poca sangre,	His veins with little blood
los ojos con mucha noche.	his eyes full of night.

Or, in 1581, he says:

y viendo que el pescador	and seeing that the fisherman
con atención la miraba,	looked at her with attention,
de peces privando al mar,	depriving the sea of fish,
y al que la mira del alma,	full of laughter she answered
llena de risa responde . . .	him who watched her from his soul

Or he says, referring to the face of a young woman:

Small door of precious coral,
clear stars of confident gaze
which you have made into crystal,
from the fine emerald and pure green . . .

Pequeña puerta del coral preciado,
claras lumbreras de mirar seguro,
que a la esmeralda fina el verde puro
habéis para viriles usurpado.

These examples come from his first poems, published in chronological order in the definitive edition of Foulché-Delbosc. If the reader continues onward, he notes that the "cultist" accent grows and grows until it completely invades the sonnets and sounds its trumpet blast in the famous "Panegyric." With time, the poet has acquired creative consciousness and has mastered the technique of the image.

Then too, I think that "cultism" is a necessity of the long line and stanza. All poets, when they write long verses (hendecasyllables or alexandrines in sonnets or octaves) try to be "cultists," including Lope, whose own sonnets are sometimes obscure. Not to mention Quevedo, who is even more difficult than Góngora, since he used not language but the spirit of language.

Short lines can be winged. The long line must be "cultist," and must weigh a lot. Remember the nineteenth century, remember Bécquer and Verlaine. In contrast, Baudelaire uses the long line, for he is a poet concerned with form. We must not forget that Góngora is essentially a plastic poet who feels the beauty of each individual line and has an unprecedented awareness for the expressive color and quality of each word. The dress of his poem is immaculate.

Clashing consonants model his lines like little statues, and his concern for architecture unites them in lovely baroque proportion. And Góngora does not want obscurity. He runs from facile expression, not out of any love of "cultism," though his was a very cultivated spirit, and not out of contempt for a crass public, though he had that in the highest degree, but rather because of a concern for scaffolding that would allow his work to resist time. A concern for eternity.

And the proof that this was a conscious esthetic principle is that before anyone else he became aware of the Byzantinism and rhythmic architecture of El Greco (another enigma for future epochs), whom he sends off to a better life with one of his most typical sonnets. Further proof of this is that he writes, defending his *Solitudes,* these bold words: "As for honor, I think that this poetry honors me in two ways; if it is read by the learned it will invest me with authority, for all must realize that through my work our language has arrived at the perfection and loftiness of Latin."

Why say more?

It is the year 1627. Ill, full of debts, hurting in his very soul, Góngora returns to his old house in Córdoba. He returns from the stones of Aragón, where the shepherds have beards as stiff and prickly as leaves of evergreen oak. He returns without friends or protectors. The Marquis of Siete Iglesias has died on the scaffold that his pride might live, and the delicate Gongoresque Court of Villamediana has fallen too, transfixed by the king's swords. Góngora's house is old and crumbling, with grates on its two windows and a big weather vane, in front of the monastery of the Discalced Trinitarians.

Córdoba, the most melancholy city of Andalusia, lives its life without secrets. And Góngora returns to her without secrets. He is a ruin now. You could compare him to an old fountain that has lost the handle of its spigot. From his balcony the poet will see dark riders on long-tailed colts; Gypsy women wearing strings of coral, on their way to wash in the drowsy Guadalquivir; gentlemen, monks, poor people who are out strolling now that the sun has gone down behind the mountains. I don't know what strange association of ideas makes me think that the three little Moorish girls of the ballad—Aixa, Fatima, and Marien—come by too, sounding their tambourines, "their color gone" but their feet agile. What do they say in Madrid? Nothing. Frivolous, gallant Madrid applauds the comedies of Lope and plays blindman's buff in the Prado. Who remembers the prebendary? Góngora is absolutely alone. To be alone in some other place might have its consolations; but what a dramatic thing, to be alone in Córdoba! He has nothing now but (as he says) his books, his courtyard, and his barber. Terrible prospect for a man like him.

The morning of May 23, 1627, the poet keeps asking what time it is. He goes to the window and sees not the landscape but a giant blue spot. A big luminous cloud hangs over the Tower of Malmuerta. Making the sign of the cross, Góngora lies down on his bed, fragrant with quince and orange blossoms. A little later his soul, well-drawn and lovely as an archangel of Mantegna, wearing sandals of gold, its amaranthine tunic flying in the wind, goes out into the street to find the ladder it will serenely ascend. When his old friends reach the house, Don Luis' hands are slowly growing cold. Beautiful, stern hands, without a jewel, satisfied with having carved the portentous baroque reredos of the *Solitudes*. The friends reflect that one should not cry for a man like Góngora, and philosophically seat themselves at the window to watch the slow life of the city. But we will read this tercet, offered him by Cervantes:

He is more pleasant, more widely admired
Yet sharper, more sonorous and grave
Than any poet Phoebus has seen.

Es aquel agradable, aquel bienquisto,
aquel agudo, aquel sonoro y grave
sobre cuantos poetas Febo ha visto.

A POET IN NEW YORK

LADIES AND GENTLEMEN:

Whenever I speak before a large group I always think I must have taken the wrong door.[1] Some friendly hands have given me a shove, and here I am. Half of us wander around completely lost, among drop-scenes, painted trees, and tin fountains, and just when we think we have found our room or tepid circle of sun we meet an alligator who swallows us alive or . . . an audience, as I have. And today the only spectacle I have is some bitter, living poetry. Perhaps I can whip its eyes open for you.

I have said "a poet in New York" when I ought to have said "New York in a poet." The poet is me, purely and simply: a poet who has neither talent nor genius, but who sometimes escapes through the looking glass of day—through its turbid bevel—more quickly than most children. A poet who comes to this auditorium wanting to imagine that he is back in his room, and that you are his friends; for there can be no written poetry unless eyes are enslaved to the obscure line, and no spoken poetry unless ears are docile and friendly. That way, the nascent word can carry blood to the listener's lips and sky to his brow.

In any event, one must speak clearly. I have not come here to entertain you—I do not want to, I couldn't care less. I am here to fight. Fight hand to hand with a complacent mass, for I am not about to give a lecture but a poetry reading—my very flesh—and I need to defend myself against the huge dragon out there who could eat me alive with three hundred yawns of his three hundred cheated heads. Now that I have come, and have broken my long poetic silence for a moment, I badly want to communicate with you. Not to give you honey (I have none), but sand or hemlock or salt water. Hand-to-hand fighting, and I don't care if I lose.

Let us agree that one of man's most beautiful postures is that of Saint Sebastian.[2] Well then, before reading poems aloud before many creatures, the first thing one must do is invoke the duende. That is the only way that everybody will immediately succeed at the hard task of understanding metaphor (without depending on intelligence or critical apparatus), and be able to hunt, at the speed of the voice, the rhythmic design of the poem.[3]

I will not tell you what New York is like *from the outside,* because New York, like Moscow, those two antagonistic cities, is already the subject of countless descriptive books. Nor will I narrate a trip, but will give my lyrical reaction with all sincerity and simplicity, two qualities that come with difficulty to intellectuals, but easily to the poet. So much for modesty!

The two elements the traveler first captures in the big city are extrahuman architecture and furious rhythm. Geometry and anguish. At first glance, the rhythm can seem to be gaiety, but when you look more closely at the mechanism of social life and the painful slavery of both men and machines you understand it as a typical, empty anguish that makes even crime and banditry forgivable means of evasion.

Willing neither clouds nor glory, the edges of the buildings rise to the sky. While Gothic edges rise from the hearts of the dead and buried, these ones climb coldly skyward with beauty that has no roots and no yearning, stupidly sure of themselves and utterly unable to conquer or transcend, as does spiritual architecture, the always inferior intentions of the architect. There is nothing more poetic and terrible than the skyscrapers' battle with the heavens that cover them. Snow, rain, and mist set off, wet, and hide the vast towers, but those towers, hostile to mystery, blind to any sort of play, shear off the rain's tresses and shine their three thousand swords through the soft swan of the mist.

It only takes a few days before you get the impression that that immense world has no roots, and you understand why the seer Edgar Poe had to hug mystery so close to him and let friendly intoxication boil in his veins.

Wandering alone, I evoked my childhood like this.[4]

Your Childhood in Menton

Yes, your childhood, fable of fountains now.—Jorge Guillén

Yes, your childhood, fable of fountains now.
The train and the woman who fills the sky.
Your shy loneliness in hotels
and pure mask of another sign.
It is the childhood of the ocean and your silence
where the wise glasses were breaking.
It is your stiff ignorance where
my torso was bounded by the fire.
I gave you a norm of love, man of Apollo,
lament with estranged nightingale,
but, feed for ruin, you honed yourself
for short, indecisive dreams.
Thought in front, light of yesterday,
indexes and signals of perhaps.
Your waist of restless sand
heeds only the footsteps which do not climb.
But I must search the corners
for your lukewarm soul which is without you and
    does not understand you,
with the pain of captured Apollo
I have broken the mask you wear.
There, lion, there, fury of the sky,
I will let you graze on my cheeks.
There, blue horse of my madness,
pulse of the nebula and of the minute hand,
I must look for scorpions' stones
and the dresses of your childlike mother.
Midnight's sobbing and the broken cloth
that took moon from the corpse's temple.
Yes, your childhood, fable of fountains now.
Strange soul of my hollow of veins,
I must search for you small and rootless.
Love of ever, love, love of never!
Yes! I want. Love, love! Let me.
O cover not my mouth, you who search
the snow for ears of Saturn's wheat

or castrate animals for a heaven
the clinic and forest of anatomy.
Love, love, love. The childhood of the ocean.
Your lukewarm soul which is without you and does
    not understand you.
Love, love, the roe's flight
over the endless breast of white.
And your childhood, love, and your childhood.
The train and the woman who fills the sky.
Nor air nor leaves nor you nor I.
Yes, your childhood, fable of fountains now.

Tu Infancia en Menton

Sí, tu niñez ya fábula de fuentes.—Jorge Guillén

Sí, tu niñez ya fábula de fuentes.
El tren y la mujer que llena el cielo.
Tu soledad esquiva en los hoteles
y tu máscara pura de otro signo.
Es la niñez del mar y tu silencio
donde los sabios vidrios se quebraban.
Es tu yerta ignorancia donde estuvo
mi torso limitado por el fuego.
Norma de amor te di, hombre de Apolo,
llanto con ruiseñor enajenado,
pero, pasto de ruina, te afilabas
para los breves sueños indecisos.
Pensamiento de enfrente, luz de ayer,
índices y señales del acaso.
Tu cintura de arena sin sosiego
atiende solo rastros que no escalan.
Pero yo he de buscar por los rincones
tu alma tibia sin ti que no te entiende,
con el dolor de Apolo detenido
con que he roto la máscara que llevas.
Allí, león, allí furia del cielo,
te dejaré pacer en mis mejillas;
allí, caballo azul de mi locura,

pulso de nebulosa y minutero,
he de buscar las piedras de alacranes
y los vestidos de tu madre niña,
llanto de media noche y paño roto
que quitó luna de la sien del muerto.
Sí, tu niñez ya fábula de fuentes.
Alma extraña de mi hueco de venas,
te he de buscar pequeña y sin raíces.
¡Amor de siempre, amor, amor de nunca!
¡Oh, sí! Yo quiero. ¡Amor, amor! Dejadme.
No me tapen la boca los que buscan
espigas de Saturno por la nieve
o castran animales por un cielo,
clínica y selva de la anatomía.
Amor, amor, amor. Niñez del mar.
Tu alma tibia sin ti que no te entiende.
Amor, amor, un vuelo de la corza
por el pecho sin fin de la blancura.
Y tu niñez, amor, y tu niñez.
El tren y la mujer que llena el cielo.
Ni tú, ni yo, ni el aire, ni las hojas.
Sí, tu niñez ya fábula de fuentes.

1910 (Intermezzo)

Those eyes of mine of nineteen hundred ten
did not see the burial of the dead,
nor the bazaar of ash of the man crying in the night
nor the trembling heart, cornered like a seahorse.

Those eyes of mine of nineteen hundred ten
saw the white wall where little girls peed,
the bull's snout, the poisonous mushroom,
and an incomprehensible moon that shone into corners and lit up
pieces of dry lemon under the hard black of bottles.

Those eyes of mine were on the pony's neck,
on the pierced breast of Saint Rose, fast asleep,

on love's tile terrace, with whimpers and fresh hands,
in a garden where the cats were eating the frogs.

Attic where the old dust convokes statues and mosses,
boxes keeping the silence of eaten crabs,
where the dream was colliding with its reality.
There, those little eyes of mine.

Ask me nothing. I have seen that things
when they seek their course find their emptiness.
There is a pain of voids in the deserted air
and clothed creatures are in my eyes—and not one nude!

1910 (Intermedio)

Aquellos ojos míos de mil novecientos diez
no vieron enterrar a los muertos,
ni la feria de ceniza del que llora por la madrugada,
ni el corazón que tiembla arrinconado como un caballito de mar.

Aquellos ojos míos de mil novecientos diez
vieron la blanca pared donde orinaban las niñas,
el hocico del toro, la seta venenosa
y una luna incomprensible que iluminaba por los rincones
los pedazos de limón seco bajo el negro duro de las botellas.

Aquellos ojos míos en el cuello de la jaca,
en el seno traspasado de Santa Rosa dormida,
en los tejados del amor, con gemidos y frescas manos,
en un jardín donde los gatos se comían a las ranas.

Desván donde el polvo viejo congrega estatuas y musgos,
cajas que guardan silencio de cangrejos devorados
en el sitio donde el sueño tropezaba con su realidad.
Allí mis pequeños ojos.

No preguntarme nada. He visto que las cosas
cuando buscan su curso encuentran su vacío.
Hay un dolor de huecos por el aire sin gente
y en mis ojos criaturas vestidas ¡sin desnudo!

And then, exhausted by the rhythm of the huge luminous signs in Times Square, in the following little poem I fled from the great army of windows where not a single person has the time to watch a cloud or converse with one of those delicate breezes stubbornly sent by the unanswered sea.

Back from a Walk

Assassinated by the sky,
between the forms that move toward the serpent
and those that search for crystal,
I will let my hair grow long.

With the amputated tree that does not sing,
and the boy with the white face of an egg,

With the tiny animals with broken heads,
and the tattered water of dry feet,

With whatever has deaf-and-dumb weariness,
and, in the inkwell, the drowned butterfly,

Colliding with my face that changes every day
assassinated by the sky!

Vuelta de Paseo

Asesinado por el cielo,
entre las formas que van hacia la sierpe
y las formas que buscan el cristal,
dejaré crecer mis cabellos.

Con el árbol de muñones que no canta
y el niño con el blanco rostro de huevo.

Con los animalitos de cabeza rota
y el agua harapienta de los pies secos.

Con todo lo que tiene cansancio sordomudo
y mariposa ahogada en el tintero.

Tropezando con mi rostro distinto de cada día.
¡Asesinado por el cielo!

But you have to go out and meet the city, you have to conquer it, and not surrender to lyrical reactions without having rubbed shoulders with the crowds on the avenues and the medley of shades from all over the world. So I take to the streets, and I encounter the blacks. Every race in the world turns up in New York, but the Chinese, Armenians, Russians, and Germans keep on being foreigners. Everyone except the blacks. There is no doubt that the blacks exercise great influence in North America, and, I don't care what anyone says, they are the most delicate and spiritual element of that world. Because they believe, because they hope and they sing, and because they have an exquisite religious purity that saves them from all their dangerous present-day troubles.

If you travel through the Bronx or Brooklyn where the blond Americans live, you sense a certain deafness—people who love falls that can shut out the glance; a clock in every house; a God glimpsed only by the soles of his feet. But in the black neighborhood there is something like a constant exchange of smiles; a rumbling earth tremor rusting the nickel columns; the wounded little boy who, if you look at him long enough, will offer you his apple pie.

Many mornings I use to walk down from the university where I lived, changing from the frightful Mister Lorca of my professors into the strange "sleepy boy"[5] of the waitresses; and wanting to find out what they were thinking, I watched the blacks dance, for dance is the most unique and poignant expression of their feelings and pain. I wrote this poem.

Norm and Paradise of the Blacks

They hate bird shadow
on the white cheek's high tide,
the struggle of wind and light
in the chamber of the cold snow.

They hate the bodiless arrow,
the exact handkerchief of goodbye,
the needle that keeps up pressure and rose
in the grassy flush of the smile.

They love the deserted blue,
the wavering bovine faces,
the lying moon of the poles,
the water's curved dance on the shore.

With the science of tree trunk and trail
they fill the clay with luminous nerves;
on sands and water they lewdly skate
tasting the bitter freshness of their ageless spit.

It is in the crackling blue with neither
sleeping footprint nor worm
where the ostrich eggs are eternal
and the dancing rains wander untouched.

It is in the blue without a past,
the blue of night that fears no day,
where the wind's nude body breaks
the sleepwalking camels, the hollow clouds.

It is there that the torsos lie dreaming
beneath the gluttony of the grass,
there that the corals imbibe the ink's despair
and the sleepers erase their profiles
under the skein of the snails,
and the dance's hollow hovers over the last cinders.

Norma y Paraíso de los Negros

Odian la sombra del pájaro
sobre el pleamar de la blanca mejilla
y el conflicto de luz y viento
en el salón de la nieve fría.

Odian la flecha sin cuerpo,
el pañuelo exacto de la despedida,
la aguja que mantiene presión y rosa
en el gramíneo rubor de la sonrisa.

Aman el azul desierto,
las vacilantes expresiones bovinas,

la mentirosa luna de los polos,
la danza curva del agua en la orilla.

Con la ciencia del tronco y del rastro
llenan de nervios luminosos la arcilla
y patinan lúbricos por aguas y arenas
gustando la amarga frescura de su milenaria saliva.

Es por el azul crujiente,
azul sin un gusano ni una huella dormida,
donde los huevos de avestruz quedan eternos
y deambulan intactas las lluvias bailarinas.

Es por el azul sin historia,
azul de una noche sin temor de día,
azul donde el desnudo del viento va quebrando
los camellos sonámbulos de las nubes vacías.

Es allí donde sueñan los torsos bajo la gula de la hierba.
Allí los corales empapan la desesperación de la tinta,
los durmientes borran sus perfiles bajo la madeja de los caracoles
y queda el hueco de la danza sobre las últimas cenizas.

But this still wasn't it. What I had before my eyes was neither an esthetic norm nor a blue paradise. What I looked at, strolled through, dreamed about, was the great black city of Harlem, the most important black city in the world, where lewdness has an innocent accent that makes it disturbing and religious. A neighborhood of rosy houses, full of pianolas and radios and cinemas, but with the *mistrust* that characterizes the race. Doors left ajar, jasper children afraid of the rich people from Park Avenue, phonographs that suddenly stop singing, the wait for the enemies who can arrive by the East River and show just where the idols are sleeping. I wanted to make the poem of the black race in North America and to emphasize the pain that the blacks feel to be black in a contrary world. They are slaves of all the white man's inventions and machines, perpetually afraid that some day they will forget how to light the gas stove or steer the automobile or fasten the starched collar, afraid of sticking a fork in their eyes. I mean that these inventions do not belong to them. The blacks live on credit, and the fathers have to maintain strict discipline at home lest their women and children adore the phonograph record or eat flat tires.

And yet, as any visitor can see, for all their ebullience, they yearn to be a nation, and even though they occasionally make theater out of themselves, their spiritual depths are unbribable. In one cabaret—Small's Paradise—whose dancing audience was as black, wet, and grumous as a tin of caviar, I saw a naked dancer shaking convulsively under an invisible rain of fire. But while everyone shouted as though believing her possessed by the rhythm, I was able, for a second, to catch remoteness in her eyes—remoteness, reserve, the conviction that she was far away from that admiring audience of foreigners and Americans. All Harlem was like her.

Another time I saw a little black girl riding a bicycle. Nothing could have been more touching: smokey legs, teeth frozen in the moribund rose of her lips, the balled-up sheep's hair of her head. I stared at her and she stared right back. But my look was saying, "Child, why are you riding a bicycle? Can a little black girl really ride such an apparatus? Is it yours? Where did you steal it? Do you think you can steer it?" And sure enough, she did a somersault and fell—all legs and wheels—down a gentle slope.

But every day I protested. I protested to see little black children guillotined by hard collars, suits, and violent boots as they emptied the spittoons of cold men who talk like ducks.

I protested to see so much flesh robbed from paradise and managed by Jews with gelid noses and blotting-paper souls, and I protested the saddest thing of all, that the blacks do not want to be black, that they invent pomades to take away the delicious curl of their hair and powders that turn their faces gray and syrups that fill out their waists and wither the succulent persimmon of their lips.

I protested, and the proof of it is this "Ode to the King of Harlem," spirit of the black race, a cry of encouragement to those who tremble and doubt and sluggishly, shamefully search for the flesh of the white woman.

And yet, the truly savage, phrenetic part of New York is not Harlem. In Harlem there is human steam and the noise of children and hearths and weeds, and pain that finds comfort and the wound that finds its sweet bandage.

The terrible, cold, cruel part is Wall Street. Rivers of gold flow there from all over the earth, and death comes with it. There as nowhere else you feel a total absence of the spirit: herds of men who cannot count past three, herds more who cannot get past six, scorn for pure science, and demoniacal respect for the present. And the terrible thing is that the crowd who fills the street believes that the world will always be the same, and that it is their duty to move the huge machine day and night forever. The perfect result of a Protestant morality that I, as a (thank God) typical Spaniard, found unnerving. I was lucky enough to see with my own eyes the recent crash, where they lost various billions of dollars, a rabble of dead money that slid off into the sea, and never as then, amid suicides,[6] hysteria, and groups of fainters, have I felt the sensation of real death, death without hope, death that is nothing but rottenness, for the spectacle was terrifying but devoid of greatness. And I, who come from a country where, as the great poet Unamuno said, "at night the earth climbs to the sky," I felt something like a divine urge to bombard that whole shadowy defile where ambulances collected suicides whose hands were full of rings.

That is why I included this dance of death. The typical African mask, death which is truly dead, without angels or "resurrexit"; death as far removed from the spirit, as barbarous and primitive as the United States, which has never fought, and never will fight for heaven.[7]

[*He reads "Dance of Death."*]

And the crowd! No one can imagine just what a New York crowd is like, except perhaps Walt Whitman, who searched it for solitudes, and T. S. Eliot, who squeezes the crowd like a lemon in his poem, extracting rats, wounds, wet shades, and fluvial shades. When, in addition, that crowd is drunk, we have one of the most intense vital spectacles that can ever be contemplated.

Coney Island is a huge fair attended on Sundays in summer by over a million creatures. They drink, shout, eat, trample each other, and leave the ocean strewn with newspapers and the streets strewn with tin cans, cigaret butts, bites of food, and shoes without heels. On its way home from the fair, the crowd sings and vomits in groups of a hundred over the railings of the boardwalk. In groups of a thousand it urinates in the corners, on abandoned boats, or on the monument to Garibaldi or to the unknown soldier.

You cannot imagine the loneliness a Spaniard feels there, especially an Andalusian. If you fall they will trample you, and if you fall into the water they will bury you under their lunch wrappers.

The rumble of that terrible crowd fills the whole Sunday of New York, pounding the hollow pavements with the rhythm of a herd of horses.

The solitude of the poems I made about the crowd rhymes with others of the same style, which I have no time to read, for instance the Brooklyn Bridge nocturne and "Nightfall at Battery Place," where sailors and women, pygmies, soldiers, and policemen dance on a tired sea, a pasture for siren cows, a promenade for bells and lowing buoys.

["*Landscape of the Vomiting Crowd*"]

The month of August is here. New York is leveled by heat, Ecijan style,[8] and I have to leave for the country.

Green lake, landscape of hemlocks. Suddenly, in the forest, an abandoned distaff. I live with some farmers. A little girl, Mary, who eats maple syrup, and a little boy, Stanton, who plays a Jew's harp, keep me company and patiently teach me the list of North American presidents. When we get to the great Lincoln, they give him a military salute. Stanton's father owns four blind horses that he bought in the village of Eden Mills. The mother almost always has a fever. I run, I drink good water, and my mood sweetens among the hemlock trees and my little friends. They introduce me to the Tyler girls, penniless descendants of an old president, who live in a cabin, take photographs entitled "Exquisite Silence," and play on an incredible spinet, songs from the heroic era of Washington. They are old and very tiny and they wear trousers so the brambles won't scratch their thighs, but they have beautiful white hair and they hold hands and listen to me improvise songs just for them at the spinet. Sometimes they invite me to dinner and give me nothing but tea and some pieces of cheese, but they tell me that the teapot is genuine china and the tea is infused with jasmine. At the end of August they take me to their cabin and ask, "Haven't you noticed, autumn is almost here?" Sure enough, on the tables and spinet and all around Tyler's portrait were the yellowest, reddest, most orange maple and grape leaves I had ever seen.

In such surroundings, of course, my poetry took on the tone of the woods. Tired of New York and yearning for the least significant, poorest living things, I wrote an insectary, which I cannot read in full to you, but where I begin by asking help from the Virgin, the Ave Maria Stella of those delightful Catholic folk. I wanted to sing to the insects who spend their lives flying and singing to our Lord with their little instruments.[9]

But one day little Mary fell down a well, and they pulled her out drowned. It would not be right to tell you of the deep sorrow, the real despair I felt that day. I will leave that to the trees and the walls that saw me. At once I thought of that other girl, from Granada, whom I saw taken out of a cistern, her little hands entwined in the gaffs, her head knocking against the sides, and the two girls, Mary and the other one, became the same child, who cried and cried, unable to leave the circle of the well, in that unmoving water that never disgorges.

[*"Girl Drowned in a Well, Granada and Newburg"*]

The little girl was dead, and I could stay in the house no longer. Stanton was sadly eating the syrup his sister had left him, and the divine Tyler girls were going crazy taking photos of the autumn woods to give me as presents.

I went down to the lake, and the silent water, the cuckoo, etcetera, made it impossible to sit there. Every way I stood or sat made me feel like a sentimental lithograph below which was written, "Federico lets his thoughts wander!!!" But at last a splendid line of Garcilaso snatched away that plastic obstinacy. A line of Garcilaso:

Nuestro ganado pace, el viento espira. Our flocks graze, the wind breathes.

And this "Double Poem of Eden Mills" was born.

[*He reads.*]

Summer vacation is over, because "Saturn detains the trains," and I have to get back to New York. The drowned girl, little Stanton "the Sugar-eater," and the pantaloonistic sisters stay with me for a long time. The train runs along the Canadian line, and I feel unhappy and miss my little friends. The girl withdraws into the well, in a host of green angels, and on the boy's chest begins to sprout (like saltpeter on a moist wall) the cruel star of the North American police.

And then once again the phrenetic rhythm of New York. But it no longer surprises me. I know the mechanism of the streets and talk to people and penetrate a bit deeper into social life. And I denounce it. Denounce it because I have come from the countryside and do not believe that man is the most important thing in the world.

[*"Denouncement of New York"*]

Time passes, and this is not the moment to read more poems. We must leave New York, and I won't read the poems about the port nor about Christmas. Someday you will read them in the book, if you are interested.

Time passes, and I am already on the ship taking me away from the howling city toward the beautiful Antilles. My first impression, that that world has no roots, stays with me . . .

> For if the wheel forgets its formula,
> it can sing nude amid herds of horses
> and if a flame burns the frozen blueprints
> the sky will have to flee before the tumult of windows.

> . . . porque si la rueda olvida su fórmula,
> ya pueda cantar desnuda con las manadas de caballos:
> y si a llama quema los helados proyectos,
> el cielo tendrá que huir ante el tumulto de las ventanas.

Edge and rhythm, form and anguish, the sky is swallowing them all. No longer do towers battle clouds nor swarms of windows eat more than half the night. Flying fish weave moist garlands and the sky, like that terrible big blue woman of Picasso, runs across the sea with open arms.

The sky has conquered the skyscrapers, and from a distance New York's architecture seems prodigious and, no matter what they intended, it moves one as much as a natural spectacle, a mountain or desert. The Chrysler Building defends itself against the sun like a huge silver beak, and bridges, ships, railways, and men seem deafened and chained: chained by a cruel economic system whose neck must soon be cut, and deafened by too much discipline and not enough madness.

I was leaving New York with feeling and with deep admiration. I was leaving many friends there, and I had received the most useful experience of my life. I must thank it for many things, especially for the holograph blues and the British stamp greens given me by New Jersey as I strolled with Anita the Portuguese Indian and Sofía Megwinoff the Russian Puerto Rican,[10] and for that divine aquarium and that zoo where I felt like a child and remembered all the children in the world.

But the ship is getting farther away, and we are beginning to come to palm and cinnamon, the perfume of the America with roots, God's America, Spanish America.

But what's this? Spain again? Universal Andalusia? It is the yellow of Cádiz, but a shade brighter; the rosiness of Seville, but more like carmine; the green of Granada, but gently phosphorescent like a fish.

Havana rises up amid canefields and the noise of maracas, cornets, chinas, and marimbas. And who should come to welcome me at the port but the dark Trinidad of my childhood, that woman who always used to stroll "along the dock of Havana."[11]

And the blacks are here, with rhythms I discover are typical of the great Andalusian people—little blacks without tragedy who roll their eyes and say, "We are Latins."

Against three great horizontal lines—the line of the canefields, that of the terraces, and that of the palm trees, a thousand blacks, their cheeks dyed orange, as though running a fever of 152°, dance this "son," which I composed and which comes to us like a breeze from the island:

When the full moon comes, I will go to Santiago de Cuba
I'll go to Santiago
in a coach of black water
I'll go to Santiago
The palm roofs will sing
I'll go to Santiago
when the palm wants to be a swan
I'll go to Santiago
and the plantain wants to be wood
I'll go to Santiago
I'll go to Santiago
with the blond head of Fonseca
I'll go to Santiago
and the rose of Romeo y Julieta
I'll go to Santiago
Sea of paper, silver of coins
I'll go to Santiago
Oh Cuba, Oh rhythm of dry seeds
I'll go to Santiago
Oh hot waist and drop of wood
I'll go to Santiago
Harp of living tree trunk, cayman, tobacco flower
I'll go to Santiago
I always said I would go to Santiago

in a coach of black water
I'll go to Santiago
Breeze and liquor in the wheels
I'll go to Santiago
My coral in the dark
I'll go to Santiago
The sea drowned in the sand
I'll go to Santiago
White heat and dead fruit
I'll go to Santiago
Oh bovine coolness of the cane
Oh Cuba! O curve of sigh and mud!
I'll go to Santiago.

Cuando llegue la luna llena iré a Santiago de Cuba.
Iré a Santiago.
En un coche de agua negra.
Iré a Santiago.
Cantarán los techos de palmera.
Iré a Santiago.
Cuando la palma quiere ser cigüeña.
Iré a Santiago.
Y cuando quiere ser medusa el plátano.
Iré a Santiago.
Con la rubia cabeza de Fonseca.
Iré a Santiago.
Y con el rosa de Romeo y Julieta.
Iré a Santiago.
Mar de papel y plata de monedas.
Iré a Santiago
¡Oh Cuba, oh ritmo de semillas secas!
Iré a Santiago.
¡Oh cintura caliente y gota de madera!
Iré a Santiago.
¡Arpa de troncos vivos, caimán, flor de tabaco!
Iré a Santiago.
Siempre dije que yo iría a Santiago
en un coche de agua negra.

Iré a Santiago.
Brisa y alcohol en las ruedas.
Iré a Santiago.
Mi coral en la tiniebla.
Iré a Santiago.
El mar ahogado en la arena.
Iré a Santiago.
Calor blanco, fruta muerta.
Iré a Santiago.
¡Oh bovino frescor de cañavera!
¡Oh Cuba! ¡Oh curva de suspiro y barro!
Iré a Santiago.

ON THE GYPSY BALLADS

The man before you is neither a poet who has made himself a bit famous nor a beginning playwright yearning for great theater,[1] but a true friend and comrade who remembers like yesterday fighting it out with the enormous mustachioed face of Mercantile Law and living a life of fun and practical jokes so as to hide a true but charitable melancholy.[2]

I know very well that these affairs called "conferencias" fill the audience's eyes with the pinpoints where Morpheus hangs his irresistible anemones, and I know that they bring into theaters and lecture halls yawns that are too big for even the mouth of an alligator.

I know that the lecturer is often a pedant who does not try to get close to his listeners and who speaks on what is old hat to him, without spending energy and without force of love, until the audience is seized with such hatred it wants to see him trip on leaving the podium or sneeze so furiously that his spectacles go crashing into the water glass.

That is why I did not come here to give a lecture on some theme I studied and prepared, but to communicate with you about something no one has taught me, the substance and pure magic of poetry.

I have chosen to read and briefly comment on the *Gypsy Ballads* not only because that is my most popular work but also because until now it is my most unified one. It is there that my poetic face appears for the first time with its own personality, well sketched and virgin of contact with any other poet. I will not criticize the book nor study what it means as a form of balladry, nor show the machinery of its images, nor graph its rhythmic and phonetic development, but I will show you its sources, the first glimpses of its total conception.

Though it is called Gypsy, the book as a whole is the poem of Andalusia, and I called it Gypsy because the Gypsy is the loftiest, most profound and aristocratic element of my country, the most deeply representative of its mode, the very keeper of the glowing embers, blood, and alphabet of Andalusian and universal truth.

Thus the book is a retable of Andalusia with its Gypsies, horses, archangels, planets, its Jewish and Roman breezes, rivers, crimes, the vulgar note of the contrabandistas, and the celestial note of the naked children of Córdoba who make fun of Saint Raphael. A book that hardly expresses visible Andalusia at all, but where hidden Andalusia trembles. I will even say this: the book is antifolklore, anti-local color, and anti-Flamenco; contains not one short jacket, suit of lights, wide-brimmed hat or Andalusian tambourine; has figures of millennial depths and just one character, Pain, dark and big as the summer sky, who percolates through the bone marrow and the sap of trees and has nothing to do with melancholy, nostalgia, or any other affliction or disease of the soul, being an emotion more heavenly than earthly. Andalusian pain, which is the struggle of the loving intelligence with the incomprehensible mystery that surrounds it.

But a poetic event, like a criminal event or a juridic one, must exist in the world, must necessarily be bandied about and interpreted. And though this poem has been recited vulgarly and sensually by ignorant creatures who have a false vision of it, I do not complain. I believe that the purity of its construction and the noble tone I tried so hard to use while creating it will defend it from those who drool on it and love it excessively.

From my very first steps in poetry, in 1919, I devoted much thought to the ballad form, because I realized it was the vessel best shaped to my sensibility. The ballad had gone nowhere from the last exquisite little ballads of Góngora until the Duque de Rivas made it sweet, fluent, and domestic and Zorrilla filled it with water lilies, shades, and sunken bells.

The typical ballad had always been a narration, and it was the narrative element that made its physiognomy so charming, for when it grew lyrical without an echo of anecdote it would turn into a song. I wanted to fuse the narrative ballad with the lyrical without changing the quality of either, and this is achieved in some of the poems of the *Gypsy Ballads,* for example the "Sleepwalk Ballad," where one gets the sensation of anecdote in a poignant dramatic atmosphere and no one knows what is happening, not even me, for poetic mystery is also mysterious to the poet who imparts it, often unknowingly.

In reality, I found my own form of the ballad, or rather it was communicated to me, in the dawning of my first poems, where you can see the same elements as in the *Gypsy Ballads,* with a similar mechanism.

In 1920 I was already writing this crepuscule:[3]

El diamante de una estrella
ha rayado el hondo cielo.
Pájaro de luz que quiere
escapar del firmamento
y huye del enorme nido
donde estaba prisionero
sin saber que lleva atada
una cadena en el cuello.
Cazadores extrahumanos
están cazando luceros,
cisnes de plata maciza
en el agua del silencio.
Los chopos niños recitan
la *cartilla.* Es el maestro
un chopo antiguo que mueve
tranquilo sus brazos viejos.
¡Rana, empieza tu cantar!
¡Grillo, sal de tu agujero!
Haced un bosque sonoro
con vuestras flautas. Yo vuelvo
hacia mi casa intranquilo.
Se agitan en mi recuerdo
dos palomas campesinas
y en el horizonte, lejos,
se hunde el arcaduz del día.
¡Terrible noria del tiempo!

The diamond of a star
has scored the deep sky,
bird of light that wants
to leave the firmament,
fleeing the huge nest
where it was imprisoned,
not knowing it has
a chain around its neck.
Extrahuman hunters
stalk the evening stars,
swans of solid silver
in the stillness's water.
Boy poplars recite
their lessons and the teacher
is an ancient poplar
who quietly moves his old arms.
Oh frog, begin your song!
Oh cricket, leave your nest!
Use your flute and make
the woods resound while I
turn uneasily home.
Two doves in the fields
tremble in my memory
as the pail of day
sinks into the far
horizon: terrifying
waterwheel of Time!

Formally, at least, that poem already shows the chiaroscuro of the *Gypsy Ballads,* and the delight in mingling astronomical images with bugs and ordinary occurrences, a basic note in my poetic character.

It embarrasses me a bit to talk about myself in public, but I will do so because I consider you friends or candid listeners and because I know that a poet, when he is a poet, is simple, and when he is simple he can never fall into the comical hell of pedantry.

One can speak for a long time analyzing and observing the multiple aspects of a poem. I am going to give you a map of this one of mine, and begin reading its individual compositions.

From the very first lines, we note that myth is mixed with what we might call the "realistic" element. But in fact when this "realism" touches the plane of magic it becomes as mysterious and indecipherable as the Andalusian soul, which is a dramatic struggle between the poison of the Orient and the geometry and equilibrium imposed by the Roman and Andalusian civilizations.

The book begins with two invented myths, the moon as a deathly ballerina and the wind as a satyr. A myth of the moon over lands of dramatic dance—concentrated, religious, inner Andalusia; and a myth of the Tartesian beach where the air is as soft as the skin of a peach and all drama and dance are balanced on an intelligent needle of jest or irony.

Romance de la Luna, Luna

La luna vino a la fragua
con su polisón de nardos.
El niño la mira mira.
El niño la está mirando.
En el aire conmovido
mueve la luna sus brazos
y enseña, lúbrica y pura,
sus senos de duro estaño.
Huye luna, luna, luna.
Si vinieran los gitanos,
harían con tu corazón
collares y anillos blancos.
Niño, déjame que baile.
Cuando vengan los gitanos,
te encontrarán sobre el yunque
con los ojillos cerrados.
Huye luna, luna, luna

Ballad of the Moon Moon

The moon came to the forge
wearing a bustle of nards.
The child is looking, looking
The child is looking hard.
In the troubled air
the wind moves her arms,
showing, lewd and pure,
her hard, tin breasts.
Run, moon moon moon,
if the Gypsies came
they would make your heart
into necklaces and white rings.
Child, let me dance;
when the Gypsies come
they will find you on the anvil,
your little eyes shut tight.
Run, moon moon moon,

que ya siento sus caballos.
Niño, déjame, no pises
mi blancor almidonado.

El jinete se acercaba
tocando el tambor del llano.
Dentro de la fragua el niño,
tiene los ojos cerrados.

Por el olivar venían,
bronce y sueño, los gitanos.
Las cabezas levantadas
y los ojos entornados.

¡Cómo canta la zumaya,
ay cómo canta en el árbol!
Por el cielo va la luna
con un niño de la mano.

Dentro de la fragua lloran,
dando gritos, los gitanos.
El aire la vela, vela.
El aire la está velando.

I can hear their horses.
Child, let me be, don't walk
on my starchy white.

The rider was getting closer,
playing the drum of the plain.
In the forge the child
had shut his eyes tight.

Bronze and dream, the Gypsies
crossed the olive grove,
their heads held high,
their eyes half closed.

Ay how the nightjar sang!
How it sang in the tree!
The moon goes through the sky,
a child in her hand.

In the forge the Gypsies
wept and cried out.
The air was watching watching,
The air watched all night long.

Preciosa y el Aire

Su luna de pergamino
Preciosa tocando viene
por un anfibio sendero
de cristales y laureles.
El silencio sin estrellas,
huyendo del sonsonete,
cae donde el mar bate y canta
su noche llena de peces.
En los picos de la sierra
los carabineros duermen
guardando las blancas torres
donde viven los ingleses.

Preciosa and the Wind

Playing her parchment moon,
Preciosa comes along
an amphibious path
of laurel trees and glass.
Silence without a star
flees the throbbing sound
and falls where the ocean beats
singing its night full of fish.
On the mountain peaks
sleep the Civil Guard
watching the white towers
where the English live.

Y los gitanos del agua
levantan por distraerse,
glorietas de caracolas
y ramas de pino verde.

*

Su luna de pergamino
Preciosa tocando viene.
Al verla se ha levantado
el viento, que nunca duerme.
San Cristobalón desnudo,
lleno de lenguas celestes,
mira a la niña tocando
una dulce gaita ausente.

Niña, deja que levante
tu vestido para verte.
Abre en mis dedos antiguos
la rosa azul de tu vientre.

Preciosa tira el pandero
y corre sin detenerse.
El viento-hombrón la persigue
con una espada caliente.

Frunce su rumor el mar.
Los olivos palidecen.
Cantan las flautas de umbría
y el liso gong de la nieve.

¡Preciosa, corre, Preciosa,
que te coge el viento verde!
¡Preciosa, corre, Preciosa!
¡Míralo por donde viene!
Sátiro de estrelas bajas
con sus lenguas relucientes.

*

Preciosa, llena de miedo,
entra en la casa que tiene,

And the Gypsies of the water,
just to pass the time,
raise bowers of snails
and branches of green pine.

*

Playing her parchment moon
Preciosa comes along.
The wind, who never sleeps,
sees her and arises;
a nude Saint Christopher
full of celestial tongues
watches the child play
a sweet, absent flageolet.

Let me see you, child,
let me lift your dress.
Open in my old fingers
the blue rose of your womb.

Preciosa throws away
her tambourine and runs.
The wind giant pursues her
with a hot sword.

The sea contracts her sound.
The olive trees turn pale.
Flutes of darkness sing,
and the snow's smooth gong.

Hurry, Preciosa, hurry!
Or the wind will get you.
Run, Preciosa, run!
The wind is close behind,
satyr of low stars
with his shiny tongues.

*

Full of fear Preciosa
goes into the house

más arriba de los pinos,
el cónsul de los ingleses.

the English consul has
up above the pines.

Asustados por los gritos
tres carabineros vienen,
sus negras capas ceñidas
y los gorros en las sienes.

Frightened by her cries
come three Civil Guards,
their black capes pulled tight,
their hats pulled on hard.

El inglés da a la gitana
un vaso de tibia leche,
y una copa de ginebra
que Preciosa no se bebe.

The Englishman gives the Gypsy
a glass of lukewarm milk
and a tumbler of gin
which Preciosa does not take.

Y mientras cuenta, llorando,
su aventura a aquella gente,
en las tejas de pizarra
el viento, furioso, muerde.

And as she cries and tells
those people her adventure
on the tiles of the roof
the wind, furious, bites.

The ballad "The Brawl" (between youngsters) expresses the mute struggle latent throughout Andalusia and Spain among groups that attack each other without knowing why, for mysterious reasons—because of a look, a rose, a love affair two centuries old, or because a man suddenly feels a bug on his cheek.

Reyerta

En la mitad del barranco
las navajas de Albacete,
bellas de sangre contraria,
relucen como los peces.
Una dura luz de naipe
recorta en el agrio verde,
caballos enfurecidos
y perfiles de jinetes.
En la copa de un olivo
lloran dos viejas mujeres.
El toro de la reyerta
se sube por las paredes.

The Brawl

Halfway down the gorge
the Albacete knives,
beautiful with enemy blood
glow like fish.
In the sour green
the hard light of a card
traces raging horses
and profiles of riders.
Two old women cry
in an olive tree.
The bull of the dispute
climbs right up the walls.

Angeles negros traían
pañuelos y agua de nieve.
Angeles con grandes alas
de navajas de Albacete.
Juan Antonio el de Montilla
rueda muerto la pendiente,
su cuerpo lleno de lirios
y una granada en las sienes.
Ahora monta cruz de fuego,
carretera de la muerte.

*

El juez, con guardia civil,
por los olivares viene.
Sangre resbalada gime
muda canción de serpiente.
Señores guardias civiles:
aquí pasó lo de siempre.
Han muerto cuatro romanos
y cinco cartagineses.

*

La tarde loca de higueras
y de rumores calientes
cae desmayada en los muslos
heridos de los jinetes.
Y ángeles negros volaban
por el aire del poniente.
Angeles de largas trenzas
y corazones de aceite.

Black angels were bringing
handkerchiefs and snow water,
angels whose big wings
were Albacete blades.
Juan Antonio of Montilla
rolls dead down the slope,
his body full of lilies,
a pomegranate in his temples.
Now a cross of fire
rides the road of death.

*

Through the olive groves
come judge and Civil Guard
as the split blood moans
the snake's unspoken song.
Gentlemen of the Guard,
this is nothing new—
four Romans and five
Carthaginians died.

*

The afternoon gone mad
from hot sounds and figs
swoons and falls into
the riders' wounded thighs.
Black angels were flying
through the western sky,
angels with long tresses
and hearts of olive oil.

Next comes the "Sleepwalk Ballad," of which I have already spoken. It is one of the most mysterious in the book, and is thought by many people to be a ballad expressing Granada's longing for the sea and the anguish of a city that cannot hear the waves and seeks them in the play of her underground waters and in the undulous clouds with which she covers her mountains. That is so, but this poem is also something else. It is a pure poetic event of Andalusian essence, and will always have changing lights, even for me, the man who communicated it. If you ask me why I wrote, "A thousand crystal tambourines / were wounding the dawn," I will tell you that I saw them, in the hands of angels and trees, but I will not be able to say more; certainly I cannot explain their meaning. And that is the way it should be. By means of poetry a man more rapidly approaches the cutting edge that the philosopher and the mathematician turn away from in silence. [*He reads the poem.*][4]

The next poem in the book is the "Ballad of the Unfaithful Wife," which is very pretty, both in its form and in its images. But this *is* pure Andalusian anecdote. It is popular to the point of desperation, and because I consider it the most rudimentary, the most alluring to sensuality, and the least Andalusian, I will not read it.

Set against the swaggering, ardent night of "The Unfaithful Wife," a night of the high vega and the reed in the penumbra, we have the night of Soledad Montoya, who embodies incurable pain, the black pain we cannot get rid of except by taking a knife and opening a deep buttonhole in the left side.

The Pain of Soledad Montoya is the root of the Andalusian people. It is not anguish, because in pain one can smile, nor does it blind, for it never produces weeping. It is a longing without object, a keen love for nothing, with the certainty that death (the eternal care of Andalusia) is breathing behind the door. This poem has an antecedent in the "Rider's Song" I shall read first, which seems to picture that prodigious Andalusian Omar ibn-Hafsun exiled forever from his fatherland:[5]

Córdoba. Lejana y sola.	Córdoba. Distant and lonely.
Jaca negra, luna grande, y aceitunas en mi alforja. Aunque sepa los caminos yo nunca llegaré a Córdoba.	Black pony, big moon, and olives in my saddlebags, even though I know the roads I will not get to Córdoba.
Por el llano, por el viento, jaca negra, luna roja. La muerte me está mirando desde las torres de Córdoba.	Across the plain and through the wind, black pony, red moon, death is watching me from the towers of Córdoba.
¡Ay qué camino tan largo! ¡Ay mi jaca valerosa!	Ay, how long the road! Ay, my valiant pony!

¡Ay que la muerte me espera,
antes de llegar a Córdoba!

Córdoba.
Lejana y sola.

Ay, death awaits me
before I get to Córdoba.

Córdoba.
Distant and lonely.

Romance de la Pena Negra

Las piquetas de los gallos
cavan buscando la aurora,
cuando por el monte oscuro
baja Soledad Montoya.
Cobre amarillo, su carne,
huele a caballo y a sombra.
Yunques ahumados sus pechos,
gimen canciones redondas.
Soledad: ¿por quién preguntas
sin compaña y a esta horas?
Pregunte por quien pregunte,
dime: ¿a ti qué se te importa?
Vengo a buscar lo que busco,
mi alegría y mi persona.
Soledad de mis pesares,
caballo que se desboca,
al fin encuentra la mar
y se lo tragan las olas.
No me recuerdes el mar,
que la pena negra brota
en las tierras de aceituna
bajo el rumor de las hojas.
¡Solidad, qué pena tienes!
¡Qué pena tan lastimosa!
Lloras zumo de limón
agrio de espera y de boca.
¡Qué pena tan grande! Corro
mi casa como una loca,
mis dos trenzas por el suelo,

Ballad of the Black Pain

Pickaxes of the roosters
are mining the aurora
when down the dark mountain
comes Soledad Montoya.
Her flesh is yellow copper
that smells of horses and shade.
Smoky anvils, her breasts
weep round songs.
Soledad, who do you ask for,
alone at such an hour?
No matter who it is,
what is it to you?
I want whatever I want,
my person and my joy.
Oh Soledad of my sorrows,
horse that runs away,
finds the sea at last,
swallowed by the waves.
Do not remind me of the sea,
for the black pain springs
from lands of the olive
under rustling leaves.
Soledad, how you hurt!
Ah, what dreadful pain!
You cry lemon juice
that is sour from waiting and your mouth.
Ah, what pain! I walk
madly around the house,
from the kitchen to the bedroom,

de la cocina a la alcoba.
¡Qué pena! Me estoy poniendo
de azabache, carne y ropa.
¡Ay mis camisas de hilo!
¡Ay mis muslos de amapola!
Soledad: lava tu cuerpo
con agua de las alondras,
y deja tu corazón
en paz, Soledad Montoya.

*

Por abajo canta el río:
volante de cielo y hojas.
Con flores de calabaza,
la nueva luz se corona.
¡Oh pena de los gitanos!
Pena limpia y siempre sola.
¡Oh pena de cauce oculto
y madrugada remota!

two tresses on the floor.
Ah, what pain! My clothes
and flesh are turning black.
Alas for my linen shirts,
alas for my poppy thighs!
Soledad, wash your body
in water of the larks,
Soledad Montoya, let
peace into your heart.

*

Downstream the river sings
a veil of sky and leaves
and the new light crowns
itself in pumpkin flowers.
Oh pain, pain of the Gypsies,
pain that is clean and always alone,
pain from a hidden spring
and from a distant dawn!

Suddenly the archangels that express the three great Andalusias burst into the poem. Saint Michael, king of the air, who flies over Granada, the city of torrents and mountains. Saint Raphael, peregrine archangel who lives in the Bible and the Koran, perhaps a better friend of the Mussulmans than the Christians, and who fishes in the river of Córdoba. Saint Gabriel Archangel, the annunciator, the father of modern publicity, who plants his lilies in the tower of Seville. They are the three Andalusias that are expressed in this song:[4]

Arbolé arbolé
seco y verdé.

La niña de bello rostro
está cogiendo aceituna.
El viento, galán de torres,
la prende por la cintura.
Pasaron cuatro jinetes,
sobre jacas andaluzas,
con trajes de azul y verde,
con largas capas oscuras.

Tree, tree
dry and green.

The girl of pretty face
is picking olives.
The wind, gallant of towers,
takes her around the waist.
Four riders went by
on Andalusian ponies,
in suits of blue and green
and long dark capes.

"Vente a Córdoba, muchacha."
La niña no los escucha.
Pasaron tres torerillos
delgaditos de cintura,
con trajes color naranja
y espadas de plata antigua.
"Vente a Sevilla, muchacha."
La niña no los escucha.
Cuando la tarde se puso
morada, con luz difusa,
pasó un joven que llevaba
rosas y mirtos de luna.
"Vente a Granada, muchacha."
Y la niña no lo escucha.
La niña del bello rostro
sigue cogiendo aceituna,
con el brazo gris del viento
ceñido por la cintura.

Aborlé arbolé
seco y verdé.

"Come to Córdoba, girl."
The child does not listen.
Three little bullfighters pass,
thin about the waist,
with orange colored suits
and swords of ancient plate.
"Come to Seville, girl."
The child does not listen.
When the afternoon
spread with purple light,
a boy came by who carried
roses and myrtles of moon.
"Come to Granada, girl."
The child does not listen.
The girl of pretty face
goes on picking olives,
gray arm of the wind
wrapped around her waist.

Tree, tree
dry and green.

Because I do not have time to read the entire book, I shall read only "Saint Gabriel":

I
Un bello niño de junco,
anchos hombros, fino talle,
piel de nocturna manzana,
boca triste y ojos grandes,
nervio de plata caliente,
ronda la desierta calle.
Sus zapatos de charol
rompen las dalias del aire,
con los dos ritmos que cantan
breves lutos celestiales.
En la ribera del mar
no hay palma que se le iguale,
ni emperador coronado

I
A lovely child, a reed,
broad shoulders, fine waist,
the skin of a nocturnal apple,
sad mouth and big eyes,
nerves of hot silver,
he walks the deserted street.
His patent leather shoes
break the dahlias of the breeze
with two rhythms that sing
brief celestial dirges.
Along the shore of the sea
no palm can equal him,
and no crowned emperor

ni lucero caminante.
Cuando la cabeza inclina
sobre su pecho de jaspe,
la noche busca llanuras
porque quiere arrodillarse.
Las guitarras suenan solas
para San Gabriel Arcángel,
domador de palomillas
y enemigo de los sauces.
San Gabriel: El niño llora
en el vientre de su madre.
No olvides que los gitanos
te regalaron el traje.

II

Anunciación de los Reyes,
bien lunada y mal vestida,
abre la puerta al lucero
que por la calle venía.
El Arcángel San Gabriel,
entre azucena y sonrisa,
bisnieto de la Giralda,
se acercaba de visita.
En su chaleco bordado
grillos ocultos palpitan.
Las estrellas de la noche
se volvieron campanillas.
San Gabriel: aquí me tienes
con tres clavos de alegría.
Tu fulgor abre jazmines
sobre mi cara encendida.
Dios te salve, Anunciación.
Morena de maravilla.
Tendrás un niño más bello
que los tallos de la brisa.
¡Ay San Gabriel de mis ojos!
¡Gabrielillo de mi vida!,
para sentarte yo sueño

nor any wandering star.
When his head is resting
on his jasper breast,
the night looks for plains
because it wants to kneel.
Guitars play by themselves
for Saint Gabriel the Archangel,
the tamer of little doves,
the willows' enemy.
Saint Gabriel: the child is crying
in its mother's womb.
Don't forget, the Gypsies
gave your suit to you.

II

Anunciación de los Reyes—
beauty spots and badly dressed—
opens her door to the star
coming down the street.
Saint Gabriel the Archangel,
between white lily and smile,
great grandson of the Giralda
was coming for a visit.
Inside his embroidered jacket
hidden crickets pulse.
All the stars of the night
turned into little bells.
Oh here I am, Saint Gabriel,
with three nails of happiness.
Your radiance makes jasmines open
on my burning face.
God save you, Anunciación,
of all brown women the best,
Your child will be lovelier
than the stems of the breeze.
Joy of my heart, Saint Gabriel,
oh Gabriel dearer than life,
I dream that I will give you

un sillón de clavellinas.
Dios te salve, Anunciación,
bien lunada y mal vestida.
Tu niño tendrá en el pecho
un lunar y tres heridas.
¡Ay San Gabriel que reluces!
¡Gabrielillo de mi vida!
En el fondo de mis pechos
ya nace la leche tibia.
Dios te salve, Anunciación.
Madre de cien dinastías.
Aridos lucen tus ojos,
paisajes de caballista.

carnations for a throne.
God save you, Anunciación—
beauty spots and badly dressed—
Your child will have a mole
and three wounds on its chest.
Oh shining Saint Gabriel,
Oh little Gabriel of my heart,
down inside my breasts
warm milk is being born.
God save you, Anunciación,
mother of a hundred dynasties.
Your eyes shine like dry
landscapes of the smugglers.

*

El niño canta en el seno
de Anunciación sorprendida.
Tres balas de almendra verde
tiemblan en su vocecita.

The child sings in the bosom
of startled Anunciación.
Three balls of green almond
shake in its little voice.

Ya San Gabriel en el aire
por una escala subía.
Las estrellas de la noche
se volvieron siemprevivas.

Saint Gabriel with a ladder
climbs into the air.
All the stars of the night
turned into immortelles.

And now Antoñito el Camborio comes into the retable, one of its purest heroes, the only one in the book who calls me by name at the moment of his death. A true Gypsy, incapable of evil, like many who are now dying of hunger rather than sell their millennial voice to the gentlemen who have nothing except money, which is very little indeed.

[*He reads the two poems about Antoñito Camborio.*]

I will say only a few words about the Andalusian force, the centaur of death and hatred that is called the Amargo.

When I was eight years old and was playing in my house at Fuente Vaqueros, a boy looked in the window. He seemed a giant, and he looked at me with scorn and hatred I shall never forget. As he withdrew he spit at me, and from far away I heard a voice calling "Amargo, come!"

After that the Amargo grew inside me until I could decipher why he looked at me that way, an angel of death and of the despair that keeps the doors of Andalusia. This figure is an obsession in my poetic work. By now I do not know whether I saw him or if he appeared to me or if I imagined him, or if he has been waiting all these years to drown me with his bare hands. The first time the Amargo appears is in *Poem of the Deep Song,* which I wrote in 1921:

Dialogue of the Amargo

(Countryside)

A VOICE: Amargo.
The oleanders of my courtyard.
Heart of bitter almond.
Amargo.

(*Three youths in wide-brimmed hats arrive.*)

1ST YOUTH: We are going to be late.

2ND YOUTH: It is almost night.

1ST YOUTH: What about *him?*

2ND YOUTH: He's coming.

1ST YOUTH (*loudly*): Amargo!

AMARGO (*from far away*): I'm coming!

2ND YOUTH (*loudly*): Amargo!

AMARGO (*calmly*): I am coming.

(*Pause*)

1ST YOUTH: What beautiful olive groves.

2ND YOUTH: Yes.

(*Long silence*)

1ST YOUTH: I don't like to travel at night.

2ND YOUTH: Neither do I.

1ST YOUTH: The night was made for sleeping.

2ND YOUTH: True.

(*Frogs and crickets make the bower of the Andalusian summer. The Amargo walks with his hands on his hips.*)

AMARGO: Ay yayayay.
I asked death.
Ay yayayay.

(*The scream of his song puts a circumflex accent on the hearts of those who have heard him.*)

1ST YOUTH (*from very far away*): Amargo!

2ND YOUTH (*nearly lost*): Amargo-o-o!

(*Silence*)

(*Amargo is alone in the middle of the road. He narrows his huge green eyes and ties his corduroy jacket around his waist. He is surrounded by high mountains. His big silver watch sounds darkly in his pocket at every step.*)

(*A rider comes galloping down the road.*)

RIDER (*stopping his horse*): *Buenas noches!*

AMARGO: Peace be to God.

RIDER: Are you going to Granada?

AMARGO: Granada, yes.

RIDER: Then we'll go together.

AMARGO: It looks that way.

RIDER: Why don't you climb up on back?

AMARGO: I would, if my feet hurt.

RIDER: I am coming from Málaga.

AMARGO: Good.

RIDER: My brothers are there.

AMARGO (*peevishly*): How many?

RIDER: Three. They sell knives. It's their business.

AMARGO: May it bring them health.

RIDER: Silver and gold ones.

AMARGO: A knife is a knife. It need be no more than that.

RIDER: You are mistaken.

AMARGO: If you say so.

RIDER: Knives of gold go by themselves straight to the heart. Silver knives cut the throat like a blade of grass.

AMARGO: Aren't they used for cutting bread?

RIDER: Men break bread with their hands.

AMARGO: Yes, that is true!

(*The horse grows restless.*)

RIDER: Horse!

AMARGO: It is the night.

(*The rolling road twists the animal's shadow.*)

RIDER: Do you want a knife?

AMARGO: No.

RIDER: But look, I'm giving it to you.

AMARGO: But I do not accept it.

RIDER: You will not have another chance.

AMARGO: Who knows?

RIDER: Other knives are useless. Other knives are soft and scared of blood. The ones we sell are cold. Understand? They go in looking for the hottest spot, and stop there.

(The Amargo says nothing. His right hand grows as cold as if it were holding a piece of gold.)

RIDER: What a beauty of a knife!

AMARGO: Is it worth very much?

RIDER: But would you rather have this one?

(He takes out a gold knife whose point shines like the flame of a candle.)

AMARGO: I said no.

RIDER: Boy, climb up here with me!

AMARGO: I am not tired yet.

(The horse spooks again.)

RIDER *(pulling on the reins)*: What a horse!

AMARGO: It is the darkness.

(Pause.)

RIDER: As I was telling you, my three brothers are in Málaga. How they sell knives! At the cathedral they bought two thousand of them to adorn all the altars and to put a crown on the tower. Many a ship wrote its name on them; the poorest fishermen by the sea get light from the luster of their sharp blades.

AMARGO: How beautiful it is!

RIDER: Who would deny it?

(The night thickens like a hundred-year-old wine. The fat serpent of the South opens his eyes in the dawn, and sleepers feel the infinite desire to jump off the balcony into the perverse magic of the perfume and the distance.)

AMARGO: I think we have lost the road.

RIDER *(stopping his horse)*: Yes?

AMARGO: While we were talking.

RIDER: Aren't those the lights of Granada?

AMARGO: I don't know.

RIDER: The world is very big.

AMARGO: Because it is uninhabited.

RIDER: You said it.

AMARGO: It makes me sad. Ay yayayay!

RIDER: Because you are getting there. What do you do?

AMARGO: What do I do?

RIDER: And if you are in your place, why do you want to be?

AMARGO: Why?

RIDER: I ride this horse and I sell knives, but if I did not do so, what would happen?

AMARGO: What would happen?

(*Pause*)

RIDER: We are coming to Granada.

AMARGO: Is it possible?

RIDER: Look how the balconies are shining.

AMARGO: Yes, of course.

RIDER: Now you will not refuse to ride with me.

AMARGO: Wait a bit.

RIDER: Come on, up with you! Quick, up! We must get there before the dawn breaks. And take this knife. I am giving it to you!

AMARGO: Ay yayayay.

(*The Rider helps Amargo. The two of them take the road into Granada. In the background the mountains bristle with hemlocks and nettles.*)

Cancion de la Madre del Amargo

Lo llevan puesto en mi sábana
mis adelfas y mi palma.

Día veintisiete de agosto
con un cuchillito de oro.

La cruz. ¡Y vamos andando!
Era moreno y amargo.

Vecinas, dadme una jarra
de azófar con limonada.

La cruz. No llorad ninguna.
El Amargo está en la luna.

Song of Amargo's Mother

They carry him on my bedsheet,
my oleanders and my palm.

The twenty-seventh day of August
with a little knife of gold.

The cross. And that was that!
He was brown and bitter.

Neighbors, give me a brass
pitcher with lemonade.

The cross. Don't anyone cry.
The Amargo is on the moon.

Afterward in the *Gypsy Ballads,* and most recently at the end of my tragedy *Blood Wedding,* they weep again, I don't know why, over this enigmatic figure:

. . . with a knife,
with a little knife,
on a set day, between two and three
the two men of love were killed.

With a knife,
with a little knife
that barely fits in the hand . . .

. . . con un cuchillo,
con un cuchillito,
en un día señalado, entre las dos y las tres,
se mataron los dos hombres del amor.

Con un cuchillo,
con un cuchillito
que apenas cabe en la mano . . .

But what is that sound of skulls and leather straps over there by Jaén and in the mountains of Almería? The Civil Guard is coming. This is one of the book's strongest themes, and one of its most difficult ones, for it is incredibly antipoetic. And yet, it is not. [*Reads "Ballad of the Spanish Civil Guard."*]

To round this out I am going to read a ballad of Roman Andalusia (Mérida is Andalusian and so, on the other side, is Tetouán), where the form, images, and rhythm fit together as perfectly as building stones.

[*He reads "The Martyrdom of St. Eulalia."*]

And now the biblical theme. The Gypsies and all the Andalusian people sing the ballad of Tamar and Amnon, calling Tamar *Altas Mares* ("high seas"). From *Tamar* to *Tamare;* from *Tamare* to *Altamare;* and from *Altamare* to *Altas Mares,* which is much more beautiful.

This poem is Gypsy-Jewish, as were Joselito el Gallo and the folk who settled the hills around Granada and a certain people from the interior of Córdoba.

Both in form and intention it is much stronger than the obliquities of the ballad of the "Unfaithful Wife," but it has a more difficult poetic accent that saves it from the terrible evil eye facing all innocent, beautiful acts of Nature.

[*He reads "Thamar and Amnon."*]

A TALK ABOUT THEATER

DEAR FRIENDS:

Some time ago I made a firm promise to refuse all testimonial dinners, banquets, and parties offered to my humble person; first, because I perceived that each such event puts another brick on one's literary tomb; second, because nothing could be more forlorn than frigid discourse directed at oneself, and no moment could be sadder than one of organized, though sincere, applause.[1]

What's more, and this is a secret, I believe sheepskins and banquets are a curse, the evil eye, for the man receiving them; the curse, the evil spell that come from the lax friends who think, "Now, at last, we're done with him."

A banquet is a gathering of professional people to eat with us. It is also an unwieldy assortment of the people who care least about us in life.

What I myself would organize for poets and playwrights, instead of testimonial dinners, would be furious challenges, bold attacks—"Let's see if you've got it in you to do this!"; "I bet you can't express the anguish of the sea in one of your characters!"; "I dare you to tell of the desperation of the soldier who is an enemy of war." Demands and struggle, with a depth of stern love, temper an artist's soul. Facile praise makes it effeminate and destroys it. Though the theaters are full of fake sirens crowned with hothouse roses and audiences contentedly applaud hearts of sawdust and superficial dialogue, the dramatic poet must never forget (if he wants to save himself from oblivion) the fields of rocks, wet with the dawn, where fieldhands are suffering, nor the cock pigeon wounded by a mysterious hunter and dying amid the reeds with no one to hear its sobbing.

Having fled sirens, congratulations, and false voices, I did not accept a single testimonial dinner after the premier of *Yerma.* But I did feel the greatest happiness of my short career as a playwright on learning that the theater family of Madrid had asked Margarita Xirgu (an actress with an immaculate artistic past, a luminary of the Spanish stage, the admirable creator of the leading role) and her brilliant company to give them a special performance.

Insofar as this betokens curiosity and interest in a noble attempt at theater, I want to thank all of you most humbly and sincerely. I speak tonight neither as playwright nor poet nor even as a simple student of the rich panorama of human life, but as an enthusiastic, devoted friend of the theater of social action. The theater is an extremely useful instrument for the edification of a country, and the barometer that measures its greatness or decline. A sensitive theater, well oriented in all its branches, from tragedy to vaudeville, can alter a people's sensibility in just a few years, while a decadent theater where hooves have taken the place of wings can cheapen and lull to sleep an entire nation.

The theater is a school of laughter and lamentation, an open tribunal where the people can introduce old and mistaken mores as evidence, and can use living examples to explain eternal norms of the human heart.

A people that does not cherish and help its theater is either dying or dead, just as a theater that does not use laughter and tears to take the social and historical pulse, the drama of its people, the genuine color of their spirit and landscape, has no right to call itself theater and ought to be thought of as a casino or a place to do that horrible business called "killing time." I am not talking about anyone in particular, and do not want to hurt anyone. I am not talking about the living reality, but about the unsolved problem before us.

Dear friends, every day I hear about the crisis of the theater, and I always think to myself that the sickness is not out there before our eyes, but in the shadows of [the theater's] very essence. This is not a passing sickness, not some defect in the work, it is a radical disease of organization. As long as writers and actors are in the hands of crass commercial promoters free from literary or governmental control of any sort and entirely without criteria and guarantees, those writers and actors, and with them the whole theater, will sink a little lower each day, with no hope of salvation.

The delicious light theater of slapstick, the revue and vaudeville, which I follow with interest and delight, may be able to defend themselves and survive. But theater in verse, the historical genre, the so-called "high comedy" and the splendid Hispanic zarzuela will suffer fresh setbacks each day, for these are demanding genres where true innovation is possible; authority and a spirit of sacrifice are needed to impose them on an audience one must often loftily tame, contradict, and attack. Theater ought to impose itself on the audience, not the audience on the theater. And that is why authors and actors must shed blood if necessary to invest themselves with authority. The people in the audience are like schoolchildren. They adore the stern, austere schoolmaster who demands much and sees that justice is done, but they put cruel needles all over the chairs of the timid, flattering souls who neither teach nor allow anyone else to do so.

The public, and mind you I do not say the people, can be taught. I know they can. I heard them boo Debussy and Ravel a few years ago, but I heard an ordinary audience shower their works with applause a couple of years later. Those "authors" were imposed on them by lofty, authoritative criteria superior to their own, as were Wedekind in Germany, Pirandello in Italy, and many others.

We must do this for the good of the theater and for the glory and hierarchy of her interpreters. We must take a dignified stance, confident that it will be rewarded two times over. To do otherwise would be to tremble behind the scenes and kill the fantasy, imagination, and grace of the theater, which is always, always an art, will always continue to be a noble art, though there has been a time when they cheapened its atmosphere, destroyed its poetry, and turned the stage into a free-for-all by applying the word art to whatever anybody liked.

Yes, the theater is a supremely noble art, and you, dear actors, are artists above all else. From head to toe. Why else would you have risen to the painful, make-believe world of the boards? You are artists by occupation and preoccupation, and the word "Art" ought to be written in the auditorium and dressing rooms, before we have to write the word "Business" there instead, or some other word I dare not mention. And discipline, hierarchy, sacrifice, love.

All through my life, if I live, dear actors, I hope that you will be with me and I with you. You will always find me with the same burning love for the theater, and with an artistic moral that hungers for a work, a stage, that grow better and better. I hope to go on fighting for the independence that saves me, and whatever calumnies, horrors, and sanbenitos that are hung on my body, I will answer with a downpour of peasant laughter kept for my personal use.[2]

I do not want to give any lesson; it is I who ought to be taking one. My words are dictated by enthusiasm and confidence. I am not a dreamer, I have thought hard and coldly about what I believe. Like a true Andalusian, I know the secret of coldness, for I have ancient blood. I know that the truth is not with the man who eats his bread beside the fire and shouts "today, today, today," but with whoever serenely watches the first, distant light dawning on the field.

And I know that the people in the right are not those who fasten their eyes on the little jaws of the ticket window and shout, "Now! Now!" but those who think of tomorrow and who sense that new life will soon be hovering over the world.

GREETING TO THE CREW OF THE *JUAN SEBASTIAN ELCANO*

The Spanish frigate *Juan Sebastian Elcano* has arrived in the port of Buenos Aires, bringing in her sails all the ancient poetry of the sea.[1] Mapped by Juan de la Cosa, these seas are familiar to both their glorious patron and to present-day sailors who hear "hello" and "goodbye" spoken in Castilian along all the coasts of the New World.

People use the white handkerchief to say goodbye and the warm hand to say hello. Hands and handkerchiefs form a trembling garland along the shore of every port in the world. The handkerchief can be like a bird struggling to fly, and the hand can show something of definitive silence and friendship, but not the word, which is always less expressive and emotional than the gesture.

Between the handkerchief that sends him away and the hand that receives him lies the sailor's true greeting, both arrival and departure, both happiness and sadness, in the dark, dead waves pushing against the stone of the dock. With simplest word and deepest feeling I say hello, on behalf of the Spaniards who live in this beautiful Argentine Republic, to the sailors of the frigate *Juan Sebastian Elcano*. Salud!

CONVERSATION WITH BAGARÍA

". . . Bagaría, my friend,[1] you who have given real lyricism to the noggin of Gil Robles, you who have drawn the owl in Unamuno and the stray dog in Pío Baroja, would you kindly tell me the meaning of the snail within the pure landscape of your work?"

"You ask, Federico, the meaning of my predilection for drawing snails. Very simple. One time, when I was sketching, my mother came up to me, stared at my scribbling, and said, 'My boy, I will be dead before I ever understand how you'll support yourself by drawing snails.' Since then, I've baptized all my drawings that way. Now doesn't that sate your curiosity, subtle and profound García Lorca, you whose delicate, beautiful verse, poetry on well-tempered wings of steel, has penetrated to the very bowels of the earth? But tell me, poet, do you believe in art for art's sake? Or should art place itself at the service of the people, crying when the people cry and laughing when the people laugh?"

"Great, tender Bagaría, I shall answer your question by saying that the concept of art for art's sake would be a very cruel one if, fortunately, it were not so vulgar. No true man believes anymore in that nonsense about art for art's sake. At this dramatic moment the artist must laugh and cry with his people. He must set aside his bunch of white lilies and sink to the waist in the mud, to help those who are looking for lilies. Myself, I am driven to communicate with others. That is why I have knocked at the doors of the theater, consecrating my whole sensibility to it."

"Do you think that when poetry is engendered it brings us closer to some future life? Or does it dispel our dreams of the life hereafter?"

"That unusual, difficult question comes from the keen, metaphysical worry that fills your life, Bagaría—a worry understood only by those who know you. Poetic creation is an indecipherable mystery, like the mystery of human birth. One hears voices from goodness knows where; it is useless to speculate on where they come from. Just as I was not worried about being born, I am not worried about dying. I listen to Nature and to man and feel wonder, and I copy down what they teach me without pedantry and without giving things a meaning which I am not sure they possess. The poet has not got the roof of a prodigious café with winged music, laughter, and ineffable eternal beer. Don't worry, Bagaría, be assured that we will."

"Do you think these questions strange? They are the questions of a savage caricaturist. But you have always known me to be a savage, with many pens and few beliefs and with savage, painful material to work from. Just think, poet, the whole tragic question of life flowered in a line stammered long ago by my parents—don't you think Calderón was right to say

pues el delito mayor	Man's greatest crime
del hombre es haber nacido	was to be born.

Isn't that more correct than the optimism of Muñoz Seca?"[2]

"Your questions do not seem strange at all, Bagaría, you are a true poet, always putting the wound on the finger. I answer you with utter sincerity and simplicity, and if I don't hit the mark, if I stutter, it is only from ignorance. The quills of your savagery are angel's feathers, and behind the drum that beats the rhythm of your 'danse macabre' is a pink lyre of the sort painted by the Italian primitives. Optimism is a characteristic of one-dimensional souls, souls that do not see the torrent of tears around us, caused by things that could be remedied."

"Sensitive and humane poet, Lorca, let's stay on the subject of the life hereafter. I am repeating myself, but the subject itself is rather redundant. Do you think that those who believe in a future life will be happy in a country of souls with no carnal lips to be kissed? Isn't the silence of nothingness better than that?"

"Kind, tormented Bagaría. Don't you know that the Church speaks of the resurrection of the flesh as the great reward of the faithful? The prophet Isaiah says it in a terrific line: 'the abject bones will rejoice in the Lord.'[3] And once, in the Cemetery of Saint Martin, I saw a stone beside a niche that was empty. It was hanging from the crumbling wall like an old man's tooth, and it said: 'Here Doña Micaela Gomez awaits the resurrection of the flesh.' An idea can exist and can be expressed because we have heads and hands. No creature wants to be a shade. . . ."

"Do you think it was entirely right to return the keys of your native Granada?"[4]

"It was a terrible moment, though they say just the opposite in the schools. An admirable civilization was lost, with poetry, astronomy, architecture, and delicacy that were unequaled anywhere in the world, in order to make way for a poor, cowardly, narrow-minded city, inhabited at present by the worst bourgeoisie in all Spain. . . ."

"Don't you think, Federico, that the fatherland is nothing, that frontiers will disappear? Why should a bad Spaniard be any more of a brother than a good Chinese?"

"I am wholly Spanish, and it would be impossible for me to live outside my geographical borders. But I hate anyone who is Spanish just for the sake of being Spanish. I am everyone's brother, and I execrate the man who sacrifices himself for an abstract nationalist ideal, loving his country with a blindfold on his eyes. The good Chinese is closer to me than the bad Spaniard. I sing to Spain and I feel her in my marrow. But before that I am a man of the world, the brother of all. No, I do not believe in political frontiers. Listen, my friend Bagaría, interviewers should not get to ask all the questions; their subjects have the right to ask some too. So tell me, what is this anxiety, this hunger for the other world that bothers you? Do you really want to survive the grave? Don't you think the matter is already settled, and that man cannot do anything about it, whether he has faith or not?"

"True, it is all unfortunately true. At bottom I am an infidel hungry to believe. Disappearing forever is so tragically painful. O joy, O woman's lips, O good glass of wine, you who knew how to make me forget the tragic truth! O landscape, O light that made me forget the darkness! When the tragic end arrives, all I ask for is perduration. Bury me in a garden; then at least I'll know my next life was a fertile one. . . . My dear Lorca, I am going to ask you about two things I think are among the most precious treasures we have in Spain, Gypsy song and bullfighting. The only thing I find wrong with Gypsy song is that the words talk only about their mothers. The fathers could be struck down by lightning and they wouldn't care. And that seems a bit unjust. But, all joking aside, I think it is the great treasure of our land."

"Very few people are familiar with Gypsy music; the stuff presented in night clubs is so-called flamenco, which is degenerate Gypsy music. This really is not the place to say much about it—it would take too long and would not be good journalism. As for what you say, so amusingly, about the Gypsies only remembering their mothers, you are partly right, since they live in a matriarchy and fathers are not really fathers: they live as . . . the sons of their mothers. On the other hand, in popular Gypsy poetry there are admirable poems written with paternal feeling. But very few. As for the other great theme you asked me about, bullfighting, it is probably the greatest vital and poetic treasure of Spain, incredibly neglected by writers and painters, owing mostly to the pedagogically false education given to us, an education that the men of my generation have been the first to reject. I think the bullfight is the most refined festival in the world, it is pure drama where the Spaniard sheds his best tears and his best bile. What's more, the bullfight is the only place you can go in the certainty of seeing death in the midst of the most dazzling beauty. What would become of Spanish spring, of our blood, of our language if those dramatic trumpet blasts were to stop sounding in the ring? By temperament and poetic taste I am a profound admirer of Belmonte."

"What contemporary Spanish poets do you like best?"

"There are two masters, Antonio Machado and Juan Ramón Jiménez. The first lives on a pure plane of serenity and poetic perfection; a human and celestial poet who has already transcended every sort of struggle, the absolute master of his prodigious inner world. Jiménez is a great poet ravaged by the terrible exaltation of his 'I,' lacerated by the reality around him, stung incredibly hard by insignificant things, his ears tuned to the world, which is the true enemy of his marvelous and unique poetic soul.

"But goodbye, Bagaría. When you go back to your huts, your flowers, your wild beasts, and waterfalls, tell your fellow savages to beware of discount roundtrip tickets. Tell them not to come to our cities. Tell the wild animals you have painted with such Franciscan tenderness that they must not flaunt their beauty or, at some moment of madness, turn domestic. And tell your flowers not to be too proud. Otherwise they will be shackled and made to feed on the rotten winds of the dead."

FROM THE LIFE OF GARCÍA LORCA, POET

My life? Do I even have a life? To myself I seem still a child. Childhood emotions are still inside me, I have never abandoned them. To tell my life would be to tell what I am. One's life is always the narrative of what has gone by. But all my memories, even those of my earliest childhood, are still passionately present.

But I will tell about my childhood. It has always been solely mine, so intimately private that I have never discussed it, never wanted to analyze it. As a child I lived very close to nature. Like all children I gave every object, piece of furniture, tree, and stone its own personality. I talked with them and loved them. There were some black poplar trees in the courtyard of my house. One afternoon it seemed to me that they were singing. The wind was changing notes as it went through the branches, and I imagined this was music. I used to spend hours accompanying the poplars' song. Another day I was surprised to hear someone saying my name: "Fe . . . de . . . ri . . . co . . ." I looked around but saw no one. Who was making that sound? I listened for a long while and realized that the branches of an old poplar were rubbing sadly and monotonously against one another.

I love the land. All my emotions tie me to it. My most distant childhood memories have the taste of earth. The earth, the countryside, have wrought great things in my life. Bugs and animals and country people are suggestive to only a few people. My spirit can capture their suggestiveness the same as when I was a child. Otherwise I should never have been able to write *Blood Wedding.* A love of the earth was responsible for my first artistic experience. It is a short anecdote and deserves to be told.

It was something like 1906. My homeland, a land of farmers, had always been tilled by those old wooden plows that could barely scratch its surface. That year some of the plowmen had gotten brand-new Brabante plows (the name sticks in my memory), which had won a prize at the Paris Exhibition of 1900. I was a curious little boy, and I followed that vigorous plow of ours all over the fields. I liked seeing how the huge steel prong could open incisions in the earth and draw forth roots instead of blood. On one occasion the plow hit something solid and stopped. The shiny steel blade was pulling up a Roman mosaic on which was inscribed . . . I can't remember, but for some reason I think of the shepherds Daphnis and Chloë. So that the first artistic wonder I ever felt was connected with earth. The names Daphnis and Chloë also taste of earth, and of love. My first emotions are tied to the land, the working of the fields. That is why I have an "agrarian complex," as the psychoanalysts would say.

Without this love of the land I could not have begun my next work, *Yerma.* To me the earth is profoundly suggestive of poverty, and I love poverty above all things, not the sordid poverty of hunger, but blessed, humble poverty, simple as black bread. . . .

I cannot stand old people. It is not that I hate them or fear them, they just make me uneasy. I cannot talk to them. I do not know what to say. Above all, I mean those old people who think that just by being old they are in on all of life's secrets. What they call "experience" and talk so much about I just cannot conceive of. At a gathering of old men I would not be able to say one word. Those squinty, tearful gray eyes, those twitching lips, those paternal smiles terrify me, and their affection is as unwanted as would be a rope pulling us toward an abyss. That is what old people are—the ligature, the rope between youth, and the abyss of death.

Death! She insinuates herself into everything. Repose, silence, serenity are apprenticeships. Death is everywhere. She is the great conqueror. Death begins when we are resting. Next time you are at a party, serenely talking, take a look at everybody's shoes. You will see them resting, horribly resting. You will see that they are dumb, somber, expressionless things, utterly useless and already about to die. Boots and feet, when they are resting, obsess me with their deathliness. I look at a pair of resting feet—resting in that tragic way that only feet can learn—and I think, "Ten, twenty, forty years more and their repose will be absolute. Or maybe in a few minutes. Maybe in an hour. Death is already in them."

I can never lie in bed with my shoes on, as some dolts do when they take a nap. I look at my feet and the feeling of death begins to choke me. To look at the soles of somebody's feet as they rest on their heels reminds me of the corpses I saw when I was a child. Their feet were always like that, close together, resting, in their new shoes . . . so much for death.

If suddenly I lost all my friends, if I were surrounded by hatred and envy, I could not triumph. I would not even fight. It matters little or nothing to me. It only matters on account of my friends, the ones I left in Madrid and those I have made in Buenos Aires. I know they would be unhappy if one of my works were jeered. I would suffer because of my friends, not because of my work. It is they who have obliged me to triumph. I triumph because I want them not to lose the love and faith they have placed in me. Artistically, I do not worry at all about people who do not love me or whom I do not know.

My most moving experience? It happened just yesterday, here in Buenos Aires. A woman came to the theater asking for me. She was very poor, she lives in one of the barrios. She had learned in the newspaper of my arrival. I simply could not imagine what she wanted, and I waited for her to speak. She pulled some papers from her pocket and carefully unwrapped something. She looked into my eyes and smiled, as though remembering something. "Federico . . . well who would have thought . . . Federico . . ." And when she had unwrapped her little package she took out an old, yellow photograph, the portrait of a baby. And this portrait was my most moving experience.

"Do you know him, Federico?"

"No."

"It is you, when you were a year old. I saw you being born. I lived near your parents' house. That day, the day you were born, my husband and I were going to a party. We missed the party because your mother was sick. I helped out. And you were born. This picture was taken when you were one year old. See how the cardboard is ripped? Your little hands did that when the photo was new. You broke it . . . the rip in the photo is such a wonderful souvenir for me."

That is what the woman said, and she left me speechless. I wanted to cry, to hug her, to kiss the photo, and all I could do was stare at the rip in the cardboard. There it was, my first work. I do not know whether it was good or bad, but it was mine . . .

See that? (He points to a poster.) You cannot imagine how it shames me to see my name printed in such huge letters and exposed to the public. I feel as if I am naked, in front of crowds of curious people. I just cannot stand the exhibition of my name. I ought not to mind, for that is what the theater demands. The first time I saw my name treated that way was in Madrid. My friends called me, happily announcing that I was on the road to fame. But it did not seem so nice to me. My name was on every street corner, facing the indifference of some and the curiosity of others. That was *my name,* and there it was, pasted up for all the world to use. And while that might have made a lot of other people happy, it caused me deep pain. It was as though I had ceased being me. As though a second person were unfolding inside me. An enemy to stare at me from those posters and laugh at my timidity. But, my friend, that is something I cannot help.

NOTES TO THE TEXT

(Except where otherwise indicated in the notes, I have translated from the 19th edition of Lorca's *Obras completas*. Madrid, Aguillar, 1974, abbreviated below as O.C.)

Non, non. C'est mieux la beauté que le talent.—MARÍA BLANCHARD

ELEGY FOR MARÍA BLANCHARD.

1 "Elegía a María Blanchard" was read at a memorial gathering in 1932 at the Ateneo de Madrid. I have translated from the manuscript which Lorca gave to Josefina de la Serna.

María Blanchard (1881–1932) was born María Gutiérrez Cueto in Santander. In 1903–13 she worked in Paris, and two years later, she, Diego Rivera, and others gave Madrid its first, unwanted exhibition of Cubist painting. In 1917 she sold all of her Cubist paintings and began to depict the misery around her—the lonely, the sick, the disenchanted. The contours in these works are clean and pure, the colors burn—they are, as Lorca said, "a stylized world of pain." She tried to teach art in Salamanca, was ridiculed by her pupils for her physical deformity, and, remarking that "Spain is the only country were somebody like me is made fun of," returned forever to Paris. Toward the end of her life she became a fervent Catholic and tried to enter a convent.

Some of her works are in the Musée de la Ville, Paris, and the Museo del Arte Contemporáneo, Madrid.

[2] Touching a cripple with one's lottery ticket was thought to bring good luck.

[3] "Nicanor who plays the drum"—a toy hawked at village fairs. When his string is pulled, he raises his shoulders, lowers his head, and beats a drum.

[4] There are hands like this one throughout Lorca's work. In *Impressions and Landscapes* wheatfields tremble "beneath the hand of the wind." In "Arbolé arbolé" the "gray arm of the wind" takes a girl round the waist. In "Total" the "hand of the breeze caresses the face of the sky." In the lecture on lullabies a hand tames the little horses dancing in the child's eyes. In *Mariana Pineda* an "invisible hand" pulls off the heroine's wedding ring. Near the end of his life the poet asks for a hand, "a wounded hand, if possible," to preside over his death. The hand actually comes on stage to take the child to the other world in *When Five Years Have Passed.*

[5] This is an old Christian image. Cf. the Spaniard Prudentius (348–415) on St. Eulalia (subject of one of the *Gypsy Ballads*):

> Suddenly a dove flew
> out of the martyr's mouth, white as snow,
> and rose toward the stars.
> This was the soul of Eulalia,
> swift, milky, innocent.
>
> (*Peristephanon,* III, 161–65)

[6] The Spanish for "colon" (:) is "dos puntos"—"two points." Lorca is beginning to dictate a letter.

ON LULLABIES.

[1] "Las nanas infantiles" was first given in 1928 in Madrid and repeated at Vassar College in 1930.

From a letter written in 1928: "I have been working on the 'Ode to the Most Holy Sacrament' and preparing the lecture I shall soon give at the Residencia de Estudiantes on 'the emotions of the Spanish cradle song,' an extremely difficult matter, for nothing has ever been written about it and there are infinite problems . . ."

[2] The saffron might symbolize Toledo, and "recumbent mode" ("modo yacente") suggests the carved figures on sarcophaguses and seems to mean the Castilian tableland.

[3] "Cogollo," translated as "the most succulent part," literally means the heart of a head of lettuce or cabbage. Perhaps Lorca means Switzerland.

[4] Characters in popular ballads.

[5] In a letter (July 1924) Lorca tells of the great poet's visit to Granada:

"We talked a long while about fairies, and it was all I could do not to show him the water sprites; that would have been too much for him." Jiménez had returned from America in 1916.

[6] When a reporter asked him in 1928 what games he had enjoyed playing as a child, Lorca said: "the ones played by children who are going to turn out to be complete idiots, i.e. poets: saying Mass, making altars, building little stages . . ."

[7] See Introduction, p. xii.

[8] The "papo," "bute," "marimanta," and "coco" are Spanish goblins. The coco is dark and hairy (see the etymology of coconut). The poet writes in *Impressions and Landscapes* (1918) that people on the Albaicín invent legends of duendes and marimantas "who come out at midnight when there is no moon, roam the alleys, and are seen by superstitious midwives or streetwalkers."

[9] I thank Mrs. Hildegard Marsden for the text of this lullaby:

Schlaf, Kindchen, schlaf!
Da draussen stehn zwei Schaf',
ein schwarzes und ein weisses,
und wenn das Kind nich schlafen will,
so kommt des schwarze und beisst es.
Schlaf, Kindchen, schlaf!

(Sleep, baby, sleep! Outside there are two sheep, a black one and a white one, and if the child won't sleep, the black one will come and bite him. Sleep, baby, sleep.)

[10] Lorca transforms this lullaby and uses it in Act I, Scene II of *Blood Wedding.* Also, it has sometimes been sung as cante jondo.

[11] Sung in the first scene of *Yerma.*

[12] See O.C. for the melody.

[13] See Introduction, p xii.

[14] A piano arrangement by Lorca may be found in O.C.

[15] "las cruelísimas maromas de los barcos." Does Lorca simply mean that Asturian women often help their husbands on the docks?

[16] Flora, goddess of flowering plants and a symbol of licentiousness, is confounded with Eve.

DEEP SONG.

[1] "Importancia histórica y artística del primitivo canto andaluz llamado cante jondo." In order to save deep song from commercial adulteration and extinction, Lorca and Manuel de Falla organized an unprecedented amateur agon at the Alhambra in June 1922. Lorca gave this lecture to awaken public interest.

[2] Antonio Fernández Grilo (1845–1906), a stupefying poetaster.

[3] The Vela is a bell in the tower of Granada Cathedral rung at intervals to regulate irrigation of the farmland, called the "vega."

[4] The liturgical rite called "Chant and Dance of the Sibyl" has sometimes been performed in the Seville Cathedral. Heraclitus' fragment on Cassandra sounds like Lorca on the cantaora: "with inspired lips she utters words that are mirthless, without ornament and without perfume, but through the power of the god her voice reaches across a thousand years." See also p. 49.

[5] Lorca uses this song in *The Billy Club Puppets,* Scene II.

[6] Sung by the heroine in Act I, Scene VII of *Mariana Pineda.*

[7] This is probably Ibn Sa'īd al-Magribi (d. 1274), who compiled an anthology which his Spanish translator calls "the last testament of Arabic Andalusian poetry." Perhaps Siraj-al-Warak is Ibin al-Warraq, the medieval poet. Lorca was quoting here and in the following poems from translations far removed from the originals.

[8] The image comes from an old siguiriya which Silverio might have sung:

Yo no sé por donde	I don't know
al espejito donde me miraba	what happened to the mercury
se le fue el azogue.	in the mirror I once used.

PLAY AND THEORY OF THE DUENDE.

[1] "Juego y teoría del duende" was first given in Buenos Aires in 1933. I have translated from the typewritten manuscript, corrected by the poet, in the Lorca family archives.

[2] See Introduction, p. xii.

[3] Manuel Torre (1878–1936?) was one of the first cantaores to sing cante jondo in a natural voice—from the chest, not from the throat. When Lorca met him in December 1927, he heard Torre say, "What you must search for, and find, is the black torso of the Pharaoh." (Torre was a Gypsy and thus thought himself an Egyptian refugee.)

[4] See Eckermann's *Conversations with Goethe* (entries for February 28 and March 2, 1831) and Part IV, Book XX of Goethe's autobiography.

[5] Silverio is Silverio Franconetti y Aguilar, a cantaor born of Italian parents in Seville in 1834. "The dense honey of Italy / and our own lemon / were in his deep weeping," Lorca says in a poem. The siguiriya is a form of deep song whose words fall in tercets or quatrains of 6-6-11-6 syllables.

[6] "Cuchillo" is both "knife" and "each of the six feathers of a falcon's wing, adjacent to the main feather, called the scissor."

[7] From the traditional ballad that begins, "Pascábase Marbella. . . ."

[8] From the Salamancan folksong "Los mozos de Monleon." See the O.C. for Lorca's piano arrangement.

[9] "una barandilla de flores de salitre." Here Lorca seems to remember the balustrade in Goya's fresco in the Church of San Antonio de la Florida,

Madrid. As for "salitre" (saltpeter), in *A Poet in New York* we find the odd sentence, "On the chest of the little boy begins to sprout, as saltpeter does on a moist wall, the cruel star of the North American police." And in an early letter Lorca tells a friend that the latter's literary vocation is growing in him "just as those weightless vegetations of saltpeter float on the walls of neglected houses." Such passages suggest that Lorca means not gunpowder but wall saltpeter (calcium nitrate).

10 I.e., Act 21 of *La Celestina.*

11 From the traditional "Romance del palmero" ("Pilgrim's Ballad").

12 From the Barbieri songbook.

13 "A San Andres de Teixido vai de morto o que no fuoi de vivo," says a Galician proverb: whoever does not visit San Andrés while living must do so after death. The dead crawl to the sanctuary (10 km. from La Coruña) in the form of reptiles and insects.

14 On All Soul's Day, November 2.

15 A religious procession in the Catalan town of Tortosa on the eve of Palm Sunday. There is a firsthand account, with music, in Felipe Pedrell's *Cancionero popular español.*

16 The trumpets that blast open the bullfight season and every corrida thereafter.

17 Lorca refers to Juan de Herrera (1530–1597), architect of the Escorial, mentioned earlier.

18 Lorca means the seven lagoons of Ruidera, the oasis in La Mancha where Don Quixote descended to the Cave of Montesinos. The soporific anemones allude to the satirical *Sueños ("Dreams")* of Quevedo.

HOLY WEEK IN GRANADA.

1 "Semana santa en Granada" was read over the radio in April 1936, a few months before Lorca's death in Granada.

SUN AND SHADE.

1 "Sol y sombra" was to have formed part of a book on the bullfight, which Lorca never finished. Its date of composition is uncertain. The first sentence refers to an illustration in the original manuscript.

THE POETIC IMAGE OF DON LUIS DE GÓNGORA.

1 "La imagen poética de Don Luis de Góngora" was given in Granada and Madrid in 1926–27 (on the three hundredth anniversary of Góngora's death) and again in Cuba in 1930. Lorca let it be published in 1932, but said he had changed his mind about Góngora. I have translated from the manuscript in the Lorca family archives.

2 Most of the translations from Góngora are by Edward Meryon Wilson

(*The Solitudes of Don Luis de Góngora*: New York, Cambridge University Press, 1965).

A POET IN NEW YORK.

[1] "Un poeta en Nueva York" was given repeatedly between 1931 and 1935. The poems themselves were not published until 1940. I have translated from the manuscript in the Lorca family archives.

[2] Saint Sebastian was an important image to Lorca. In 1926 he was writing three lectures about paintings of the martyrdom of Sebastian, but these have been lost. He wrote to Jorge Guillén that same year that true poetry is "love, effort, and *renunciation.* (Saint Sebastian)." Here he seems to be saying, "We must make ourselves extremely vulnerable."

[3] There is a lacuna here. Lorca probably gave his ideas on the duende.

[4] I have not thought it necessary to include the text of all the poems cited in the manuscript, which gives the titles only. The reader may consult the excellent translations of Robert Bly (Beacon Press, 1973), those of Ben Belitt (Grove Press, 1955), and *The Selected Poems of Federico García Lorca* (New Directions, 1955). The best text in Spanish is that found in Rolfe Humphries' *The Poet in New York and Other Poems of Federico García Lorca* (W. W. Norton, 1955).

[5] In English in the original.

[6] In an interview a year later Lorca said that he saw six suicides.

[7] Following the word "resurrexit" in the manuscript, but deleted: "death of Protestants who think they do not need to fight for heaven, for all is done and will always be the same."

[8] He refers to Ecija, the "Frying Pan of Andalusia," a town in Seville province on the bank of the Genil.

[9] Only part of this poem, titled "Luna y panorama de los insectos," is given in O.C. The rest is still unpublished.

[10] Sofía Megwinoff de Lanza, who was then a student at Columbia.

[11] This folksong says:

> Por el muelle de la Habana
> paseaba una mañana
> la morena Trinidad

("along the dock of Havana one morning, dark Trinidad went walking.")

ON THE GYPSY BALLADS.

[1] "[Lectura de] *Romancero gitano*" was given repeatedly in 1935 and 1936. Published in 1928, the *Gypsy Ballads* had become the most widely read modern poems in Spain.

[2] Mostly to please his parents, Lorca took a law degree at the University of Granada in 1923.

[3] "The Diamond," written in 1920 and included in *Libro de poemas* (*"Book of Poems"*), 1921.

[4] It has not been possible to include all the poems here read by Lorca. The ones omitted have already been translated well by Roy Campbell, Robert Bly, and Rolfe Humphries, while many are also included in *The Selected Poems of Federico García Lorca.*

[5] From *Canciones (1921–1924) ("Songs").*

A TALK ABOUT THEATER.

[1] "Charla sobre teatro." Realizing that *Yerma* was an extraordinary play bringing new life to the Spanish stage, the actors and actresses of Madrid asked its leading lady Margarita Xirgu to give them a special performance, late at night when their own shows were over. Lorca agreed and read these lines to "the whole theater family of Madrid" at the Teatro Español on February 2, 1935. I have translated from the text given in the *Heraldo de Madrid* of that date.

[2] Some of the reviewers had found *Yerma* "immoral" and "unnecessarily crude," and Lorca had been attacked by the conservative press for his political views.

GREETING TO THE CREW
OF THE "JUAN SEBASTIAN ELCANO."

[1] "Salutación a los marinos del Juan Sebastian Elcano" was read to the crew of the Spanish school ship when it called in Buenos Aires around Christmas 1933.

CONVERSATION WITH BAGARIA.

[1] "Diálogos de un caricaturista salvaje" appeared in the Madrid daily *El Sol* on June 10, 1936. I have translated from that text, omitting several paragraphs. Luis Bagaría (1882–1940), the most mordant and most talented cartoonist of his day, drew most of his subjects as animals and styled himself "The Savage Caricaturist.' Bored with success, he persuaded the editors of *El Sol* to let him try interviewing.

[2] Pedro Muñoz Seca (1881–1936), a facile playwright who was murdered by the Republicans in Madrid three months after Lorca was shot in Granada.

[3] Perhaps Lorca is thinking of chapter 37 of Ezekiel.

[4] Bagaría refers to Boabdil's surrender to the Catholic monarchs in January 1492.

FROM THE LIFE OF GARCÍA LORCA, POET.

[1] Excerpts from an article, "La Vida de García Lorca, Poeta," by José R. Luna in *Crítica,* Buenos Aires, March 10, 1934.

Some New Directions Paperbooks

Walter Abish, *Alphabetical Africa*. NDP375.
In the Future Perfect. NDP440.
Minds Meet. NDP387.
Illangô Adigal, *Shilappadikaram*. NDP162.
Alain, *The Gods*. NDP382
David Antin, *Talking at the Boundaries*. NDP388.
G. Apollinaire, *Selected Writings*.† NDP310.
Djuna Barnes, *Nightwood*. NDP98.
Charles Baudelaire, *Flowers of Evil*.† NDP71,
Paris Spleen. NDP294.
Martin Bax, *The Hospital Ship*. NDP402.
Gottfried Benn, *Primal Vision*.† NDP322.
Wolfgang Borchert, *The Man Outside*. NDP319.
Jorge Luis Borges, *Labyrinths*. NDP186.
Jean-Francois Bory, *Once Again* NDP256.
E. Brock, *The Blocked Heart*. NDP399.
Here. Now. Always. NDP429.
The Portraits & The Poses. NDP360.
The River and the Train. NDP478.
Buddha, *The Dhammapada*. NDP188.
Frederick Busch, *Domestic Particulars*. NDP413.
Manual Labor. NDP376.
Ernesto Cardenal, *Apocalypse & Other Poems*.
NDP441. In Cuba. NDP377.
Hayden Carruth, *For You*. NDP298.
From Snow and Rock, from Chaos. NDP349.
Louis-Ferdinand Céline,
Death on the Installment Plan NDP330.
Guignol's Band. NDP278.
Journey to the End of the Night. NDP84.
Jean Cocteau, *The Holy Terrors*. NDP212.
The Infernal Machine. NDP235.
M. Cohen, *Monday Rhetoric*. NDP352.
Robert Coles, *Irony in the Mind's Life*. NDP459.
Cid Corman, *Livingdying*. NDP289.
Sun Rock Man. NDP318.
Gregory Corso, *Elegiac Feelings*. NDP299.
Happy Birthday of Death. NDP86.
Long Live Man. NDP127.
Robert Creeley, *Hello*. NDP451.
Later. NDP488.
Edward Dahlberg, *Reader*. NDP246.
Because I Was Flesh. NDP227.
Osamu Dazai, *The Setting Sun*. NDP258.
No Longer Human. NDP357.
Coleman Dowell, *Mrs. October* . . . NDP368.
Too Much Flesh and Jabez. NDP447.
Robert Duncan, *Bending the Bow*. NDP255.
The Opening of the Field. NDP356.
Roots and Branches. NDP275.
Dutch "Fiftiers," *Living Space*. NDP493.
Richard Eberhart, *Selected Poems*. NDP198.
E. F. Edinger, *Melville's Moby-Dick*. NDP460.
Russell Edson, *The Falling Sickness*. NDP389.
Wm. Empson, *7 Types of Ambiguity*. NDP204.
Some Versions of Pastoral. NDP92.
Wm. Everson, *Man-Fate*, NDP369.
The Residual Years. NDP263.
Lawrence Ferlinghetti, *Her*. NDP88.
A Coney Island of the Mind. NDP74.
The Mexican Night. NDP300.
Open Eye, Open Heart. NDP361.
The Secret Meaning of Things. NDP268.
Starting from San Francisco. NDP220.
Tyrannus Nix?. NDP288.
Unfair Arguments . . . NDP143
Who Are We Now? NDP425.
F. Scott Fitzgerald, *The Crack-up*. NDP54.
Robert Fitzgerald, *Spring Shade*. NDP311.
Gustave Flaubert, *Dictionary*. NDP230.
Gandhi, *Gandhi on Non-Violence*. NDP197.
Goethe, *Faust*, Part I. NDP70.
Allen Grossman, *The Woman on the Bridge Over the Chicago River*. NDP473.
John Hawkes, *The Beetle Leg*. NDP239.
The Blood Oranges. NDP338.
The Cannibal. NDP123.
Death Sleep & The Traveler. NDP393.
The Innocent Party. NDP238.
The Lime Twig. NDP95.
The Owl. NDP443.
Second Skin. NDP146.
Travesty. NDP430.
A. Hayes, *A Wreath of Christmas Poems*. NDP347.
H. D., *End to Torment*. NDP476.
Helen in Egypt. NDP380.
Hermetic Definition. NDP343.
Trilogy. NDP362.
Robert E. Helbling, *Heinrich von Kleist*, NDP390.
Hermann Hesse, *Siddhartha*. NDP65.
C. Isherwood, *All the Conspirators*. NDP480.
The Berlin Stories. NDP134.
Lions and Shadows. NDP435.
Philippe Jaccottet, *Seedtime*. NDP428.
Alfred Jarry, *The Supermale*. NDP426.
Ubu Roi. NDP105.
Robinson Jeffers, *Cawdor and Media*. NDP293.
James Joyce, *Stephen Hero*. NDP133.
James Joyce/Finnegans Wake. NDP331.
Franz Kafka, *Amerika*. NDP117.
Bob Kaufman,
Solitudes Crowded with Loneliness. NDP199.
Hugh Kenner, *Wyndham Lewis*. NDP167.
Kenyon Critics, *G. M. Hopkins*. NDP355.
H. von Kleist, *Prince Friedrich of Homburg*. NDP462.
Elaine Kraf, *The Princess of 72nd St*. NDP494.
P. Lal, *Great Sanskrit Plays*. NDP142.
Lautréamont, *Maldoror*. NDP207.
Irving Layton, *Selected Poems*. NDP431.
Denise Levertov, *Collected Earlier Poems*. NDP475
Footprints. NDP344.
The Freeing of the Dust. NDP401.
The Jacob's Ladder. NDP112.
Life in the Forest. NDP461.
The Poet in the World. NDP363.
Relearning the Alphabet. NDP290.
The Sorrow Dance. NDP222.
To Stay Alive. NDP325.
Harry Levin, *James Joyce*. NDP87.
Li Ch'ing-chao, *Complete Poems*. NDP492.
Enrique Lihn, *The Dark Room*.† NDP452.
Garcia Lorca, *Deep Song & Other Prose*. NDP503.
Five Plays. NDP232.
Selected Poems.† NDP114.
Three Tragedies. NDP52.
Michael McClure, *Gorf*. NDP416.
Antechamber. NDP455.
Jaguar Skies. NDP400.
Josephine: The Mouse Singer. NDP496.
September Blackberries. NDP370.
Carson McCullers, *The Member of the Wedding*. (Playscript) NDP153.
Thomas Merton, *Asian Journal*. NDP394.
Gandhi on Non-Violence. NDP197.
News Seeds of Contemplation. NDP337.
Raids on the Unspeakable. NDP213.
Selected Poems. NDP85.
The Way of Chuang Tzu. NDP276.
The Wisdom of the Desert. NDP295.
Zen and the Birds of Appetite. NDP261.
Henry Miller, *The Air-Conditioned Nightmare*. NDP302.
Big Sur & The Oranges. NDP161.
The Books in My Life. NDP280.
The Colossus of Maroussi. NDP75.
The Cosmological Eye. NDP109.
Henry Miller on Writing. NDP151.
The Henry Miller Reader. NDP269.
Just Wild About Harry. NDP479.
The Smile at the Foot of the Ladder. NDP386.
Stand Still Like the Hummingbird. NDP236.
The Time of the Assassins. NDP115.
Y. Mishima, *Confessions of a Mask*. NDP253.
Death in Midsummer. NDP215.
Eugenio Montale, *New Poems*. NDP410.
Selected Poems.† NDP193.
Vladimir Nabokov, *Nikolai Gogol*. NDP78.
Laughter in the Dark. NDP470.
The Real Life of Sebastian Knight. NDP432.
P. Neruda, *The Captain's Verses*.† NDP345.
Residence on Earth.† NDP340.
New Directions in Prose & Poetry (Anthology).
Available from #17 forward. #40, Spring 1980.

Robert Nichols, Arrival. NDP437.
Exile. NDP485.
Garh City. NDP450.
Harditts in Sawna. NDP470.
Charles Olson. *Selected Writings.* NDP231.
Toby Olson, *The Life of Jesus.* NDP417.
George Oppen, *Collected Poems.* NDP418.
Wilfred Owen, *Collected Peoms.* NDP210.
Nicanor Parra, *Emergency Poems.*† NDP333.
Poems and Antipoems.† NDP242.
Boris Pasternak, *Safe Conduct.* NDP77.
Kenneth Patchen. *Aflame and Afun.* NDP292.
Because It Is. NDP83.
But Even So. NDP265.
Collected Poems. NDP284.
Doubleheader. NDP211.
Hallelujah Anyway. NDP219.
In Quest of Candlelighters. NDP334.
Memoirs of a Shy Pornographer. NDP205.
Selected Poems. NDP160.
Wonderings. NDP320.
Octavio Paz, *Configurations.*† NDP303.
A Draft of Shadows.† NDP489.
Eagle or Sun?† NDP422.
Early Poems.† NDP354.
Plays for a New Theater. (Anth.) NDP216.
J. A. Porter, *Eelgrass.* NDP438.
Ezra Pound, *ABC of Reading.* NDP89.
Classic Noh Theatre of Japan. NDP79.
Confucius. NDP285.
Confucius to Cummings. (Anth.) NDP126.
Gaudier Brzeska. NDP372.
Guide to Kulchur, NDP257.
Literary Essays. NDP250.
Love Poems of Ancient Egypt. NDP178.
Pavannes and Divagations. NDP397.
Pound/Joyce. NDP296.
Selected Cantos. NDP304.
Selected Letters 1907-1941. NDP317.
Selected Poems. NDP66.
The Spirit of Romance. NDP266.
Translations.† (Enlarged Edition) NDP145.
James Purdy, *Children Is All.* NDP327.
Raymond Queneau, *The Bark Tree.* NDP314.
The Flight of Icarus. NDP358.
The Sunday of Life. NDP433.
Mary de Rachewiltz, *Ezra Pound.* NDP405.
M. Randall, *Part of the Solution.* NDP350.
John Crowe Ransom, *Beating the Bushes.* NDP324.
Raja Rao, *Kanthapura.* NDP224.
Herbert Read, *The Green Child.* NDP208.
P. Reverdy, *Selected Poems.*† NDP346.
Kenneth Rexroth, *Collected Longer Poems.* NDP309.
Collected Shorter Poems. NDP243.
The Morning Star. NDP490.
New Poems. NDP383.
100 More Poems from the Chinese. NDP308.
100 More Poems from the Japanese. NDP420.
100 Poems from the Chinese. NDP192.
100 Poems from the Japanese.† NDP147.
Rainer Maria Rilke, *Poems from The Book of Hours.* NDP408.
Possibility of Being. (Poems). NDP436.
Where Silence Reigns. (Prose). NDP464.
Arthur Rimbaud, *Illuminations.*† NDP56.
Season in Hell & Drunken Boat.† NDP97.
Edouard Roditi, *Delights of Turkey.* NDP445.
Selden Rodman, *Tongues of Fallen Angels.* NDP373.
Jerome Rothenberg, *Poems for the Game of Silence.* NDP406.
Poland/1931. NDP379.
Seneca Journal. NDP448.
Vienna Blood. NDP498.
Saigyo,† *Mirror for the Moon.* NDP465.
Saikaku Ihara. *The Life of an Amorous Woman.* NDP270.
St. John of the Cross, *Poems.*† NDP341.
Jean-Paul Sartre, *Baudelaire.* NDP233.
Nausea. NDP82.
The Wall (Intimacy). NDP272.
Delmore Schwartz, *Selected Poems.* NDP241.
In Dreams Begin Responsibilities. NDP454.
Kazuko Shiraishi, *Seaons of Sacred Lust.* NDP453.
Stevie Smith, *Selected Poems,* NDP159.
Gary Snyder, *The Back Country.* NDP249.
Earth House Hold. NDP267.
Myths and Texts. NDP457.
The Real Work. NDP499.
Regarding Wave. NDP306.
Turtle Island. NDP381.
Gilbert Sorrentino, *Splendide-Hôtel.* NDP364.
Enid Starkie, *Rimbaud.* NDP254.
Robert Steiner, *Bathers.* NDP495
Stendhal, *The Telegraph.* NDP108.
Jules Supervielle, *Selected Writings.*† NDP209.
W. Sutton, *American Free Verse.* NDP351.
Nathaniel Tarn, *Lyrics . . . Bride of God.* NDP391.
Dylan Thomas, *Adventures in the Skin Trade.* NDP183.
A Child's Christmas in Wales. NDP181.
Collected Poems 1934-1952. NDP316.
The Doctor and the Devils. NDP297.
Portrait of the Artist as a Young Dog. NDP51.
Quite Early One Morning. NDP90.
Under Milk Wood. NDP73.
Martin Turnell. *Art of French Fiction.* NDP251.
Baudelaire. NDP336.
Rise of the French Novel. NDP474.
Paul Valéry, *Selected Writings.*† NDP184.
P. Van Ostaijen, *Feasts of Fear & Agony.* NDP411.
Elio Vittorini, *A Vittorini Omnibus.* NDP366.
Women of Messina. NDP365.
Vernon Watkins, *Selected Poems.* NDP221.
Nathanael West, *Miss Lonelyhearts & Day of the Locust.* NDP125.
J. Williams, *An Ear in Bartram's Tree.* NDP335.
Tennessee Williams, *Camino Real,* NDP301.
Cat on a Hot Tin Roof. NDP398.
Dragon Country. NDP287.
Eight Mortal Ladies Possessed. NDP374.
The Glass Menagerie. NDP218.
Hard Candy. NDP225.
In the Winter of Cities. NDP154.
A Lovely Sunday for Creve Coeur. NDP497.
One Arm & Other Stories. NDP237.
Small Craft Warnings. NDP348.
A Streetcar Named Desire. NDP501.
Sweet Bird of Youth. NDP409.
Twenty-Seven Wagons Full of Cotton. NDP217.
Two-Character Play. NDP483.
Vieux Carré. NDP482.
Where I Live, NDP468.
William Carlos Williams.
The Autobiography. NDP223.
The Build-up. NDP223.
The Farmers' Daughters. NDP106.
I Wanted to Write a Poem. NDP469.
Imaginations. NDP329.
In the American Grain. NDP53.
In the Money. NDP240.
Paterson. Complete. NDP152.
Pictures form Brueghel. NDP118.
The Selected Essays. NDP273.
Selected Poems. NDP131.
A Voyage to Pagany. NDP307.
White Mule. NDP226.
W. C. Williams Reader. NDP282.
Yvor Winters, *E. A. Robinson.* NDP326.
Wisdom Books: *Ancient Egyptians,* NDP467. *Early Buddhists,* NDP444; *English Mystics,* NDP466; *Forest* (Hindu), NDP414; *Jewish Mystics,* NDP423; *Spanish Mystics,* NDP442; *St. Francis,* NDP477; *Sufi,* NDP424; *Wisdom of the Desert,* NDP295; *Zen Masters,* NDP415.

† Bilingual